Dear Tasha!
I hope you enjoy
each new adventure with
increasing interest. ♡
Wendy

Season's Shadows

Wendy Black Farley

Wendy Black Farley

W0010490

New Harbor Press
RAPID CITY, SD

Farley/New Harbor Press
1601 Mt Rushmore Rd., Ste 3288
Rapid City, SD 57701
www.NewHarborPress.com

Publisher's Note: This is a work of fiction. Names, characters, places, and incidents are a product of the author's imagination. Locales and public names are sometimes used for atmospheric purposes. Any resemblance to actual people, living or dead, or to businesses, companies, events, institutions, or locales is completely coincidental.

Ordering Information:
Quantity sales. Special discounts are available on quantity purchases by corporations, associations, and others. For details, contact the "Special Sales Department" at the address above.

Season's Shadows/Wendy Black Farley. -- 1st ed.
ISBN 978-1-63357-167-9

Contents

Prologue

Tallinn, Estonia, 1988

The beauty of the Gulf of Finland was on full display as the
water reflected the glow of the late afternoon sun, but
Marga had no time for her usual enjoyment of the seascape. She
would have to hurry along the two-mile journey home to be on
time for dinner.

She didn't need the sun or a watch to know the hour was late.
The rumbling in her tummy was a reminder that the radishes
plucked from her family's small garden plot for lunch were not
enough sustenance for the long afternoon, even with the addition of a morsel of goat cheese. She was dreaming of Ema's rye
bread and baked beans with bits of salt pork. Saturday night
was always the biggest meal of the week.

Parents were often late in gathering their children from the
government-sponsored pool where she was a swim instructor

and lifeguard. Her clientele felt a special privilege due to their status with the State.

Thinking about her hopes of gaining admission to Tartu University for the study of music education brought a momentary reprieve from the focus on her gnawing hunger. Her job at the pool would provide little in terms of a salary, though anything was needed and welcome. But it was a government job and provided a greater chance of an eventual university education.

Her reverie was interrupted by footsteps behind her, and she panicked. This couldn't be happening. The school from which she graduated a few weeks before had taught her only what the Supreme Soviet wanted citizens to know. But at home, under hushed tones, the real Estonia was relayed through stories about Estonian history and her family, the annual song festivals when they sang the folk songs of Estonia rather than the praises of the Soviet Union and its leaders, and the description of Estonian folk costumes.

Outside of the home, fear was a frequent emotion. She never spoke with anyone about the topics discussed with her family. No one could be trusted. Her father's family had been arrested off the streets when he was six years old and sentenced to ten years of hard labor in Siberia. It was alleged that her great aunt, a high school teacher, had notes in her classroom about the annexation of Estonia by the Soviets that alluded to the illegality of the Molotov-Ribbentrop Pact created by the Nazi's and the Soviet Union. The family also had ties to a Forest Brother. No one ever knew the real reason for an arrest because they could happen for no reason.

Marga's grandmother died in the Gulag, and her grandfather returned with her father, then a teenager, both in poor health.

Even sans discussion, there was a shared understanding that anyone could be arrested at any time.

Despite glasnost, perestroika, and Mikhail Gorbachev's declaration that Soviet countries would emerge from their backward, poverty-laden existence, only a few glimpses of change were in the air. There was heightened hope at the recent political rally, where history came alive through political words not spoken in Estonia for many decades and made even more poignant by the surroundings of the medieval architecture of Old Town Square in Tallinn. The crowd was elated and had grown on that day to 100,000. They migrated to the song festival grounds, where for two days, they sang folk songs of Estonia and flags of Estonia waved.

But her hopes that anything had changed were dashed in a moment. Terror gripped her as the footsteps continued behind her. She turned to confirm that the follower was after her, and vaguely recognized the man who was closing in on the distance between them. There was a little-known path ahead. The elevation of the craggy cliffs would lengthen her walk and make it more challenging, but if she could get enough of a lead so that he wouldn't see her turn, she would no longer worry that he was following her.

Marga made the turn and thought about this man she had seen only once. He came to pick up his two young children at the pool a few days before. He never looked at the children, who scurried to him without being asked. There were no greetings or hugs, he simply took his eyes from Marga on whom he had been staring since entering the pool area and marched the children out. She was contemplating this odd encounter when she was grabbed from behind. She tried to scream, but her mouth was covered with a cuffed hand and dirty cloth. She fought to free herself by kicking and twisting, and everything went dark.

Chapter 1

Present Day

The blustery wind created a biting swirl of snow that hurled Cori through the entrance to her condo faster than she intended, and it was as though she had to force the door closed against the unwelcome intruder. The bombogenesis made the drive from the airport long and scary. Cori wondered how a term she had come to know only recently could be occurring so often, and she thought it strange to yearn for the good old days of simple northeasters.

The nearly cross-country flight had been arduous as well. She had exhausted her playlist, read an entire book, and paid for a movie for the first time.

Cori Sellers had basked in the Arizona sun and the loving attention of her brother and sister-in-law for the Christmas holiday, and the contrast with the viciousness of the New England

New Year were making her homecoming the most dreaded she had experienced.

Amity Associates, where she was employed as a counselor, was swamped with referrals stemming from the 'Me Too' Movement. Consultants, lawyers, and counselors were tapped for the many individuals and organizations seeking assistance in the wake of disclosures.

After unpacking her makeup and other grooming items, she deposited the rest of her luggage in the laundry. She turned up the heat, made a cup of coffee, and was reaching for her cell when the ringtone from her sister-in-law sounded.

"Hey Ainsleigh. I was about to call. I'm okay. We're having 'weather,' which delayed our landing and made the drive from the airport ridiculously slow. How are you guys?"

As a life-long resident of the desert, Ainsleigh had no experience driving in snowstorms. However, her gentle nature usually found a way to sooth and empathize with an irritable individual.

"I hope you can find a way to warm up fast and shake away the fear and aggravation you must have felt. I'm so glad you're okay."

"Ainsleigh, is everything okay? You sound as though you're about to cry . . . or you have been crying." Not only did Ainsleigh's voice sound strained, but usually her brother, Roman, was the one to call and check on Cori—unless something kept him from calling.

"Cori, I wish I could tell you this in person and at a time when you're not already exhausted."

"Ainsleigh, what?"

"Roman is in the hospital."

"Why? I just left! What happened?"

"He didn't say anything until a couple of days ago when he admitted he hasn't had any energy for more than a week. We've been keeping up with his daily therapy, but he just kept losing ground. So, he called his doctor right after you left, and he was told to go directly to the hospital."

Cori was frantic but tried not to let it show in her voice. "Are they doing anything to help?"

"They are. They said he should have gone to the hospital sooner. Cori, they are thinking about the possibility of a lung transplant."

Now Cori couldn't speak. She was audible only as she breathed out a moan and choked back her tears. She thought of how Roman had struggled his whole life with this disease and about how hard she and her parents had worked to keep the cystic fibrosis (CF) from taking his life. She thought about how happy he had been to finally meet Ainsleigh, the love of his life, and how together they carved out a meaningful life, while helping each other fight the hand they had been dealt with their medical realities. She was aware that Ainsleigh was waiting, and she finally spoke.

"I'll come. I'll come right away."

"Cori, please listen. We wanted you to know as soon as possible even though we knew you would want to come. But that isn't what makes sense right now. You've been off work for so long and should find out more before you disrupt your life at such a busy time for you. Thank you. Really. But there just isn't anything you can do right now."

"But Ainsleigh . . ."

"Cori, of course we all would love to have you here now and all of the time. But this isn't where your life is. Please make us happy. We'll handle this, and you should come when we no longer can. Is that okay?"

"I'll think about it Ainsleigh. I know you can handle it. I just want to be there."

"I know. We knew that before we called. Just trust us. Are you okay?"

"I'm sorry for my reaction, Ainsleigh. I should be asking you that. Are you okay?"

"An hour at a time. At the most."

"I know."

"Promise me you'll call Jessalyn?"

"Yes."

"Take care, Cori. You can call Roman in an hour or so."

"Thanks, Ainsleigh. I love you both. Prayers."

Chapter 2

"Hi Cori."

"Hi Jessalyn. I've got some bad news."

"What is it?" Jessalyn was gentle.

"Jessalyn, Roman might need a lung transplant."

"Oh Cori. I'm so sorry. I'll be right there."

"No. Not in this weather. Only if the snow has stopped."

"That doesn't matter. I'm coming."

Cori thought about what a good friend Jessalyn was both in good times and bad. As a nurse, she was especially helpful in her understanding of the realities Roman and Cori experienced. She was still caught up in her jumbled thoughts of Ainsleigh's words, Roman's struggles, and Jessalyn's support when her doorbell rang.

She looked out and saw her neighbor, Mrs. B., and quickly let her in.

"Cori, are you okay dear? Can I get you anything?"

"Mrs. B. How did you know I needed anything?"

"Your friend Jessalyn called and asked me to stay with you until she could arrive. She is very worried and said you had received bad news, but she didn't explain. What is it dear?"

"I just returned from visiting Roman and Ainsleigh. I barely came through the door when I received the news from Ainsleigh that, not only is Roman feeling weak and is in the hospital, but they're also discussing a possible need for a lung transplant."

"Oh dear. No wonder you're upset. This must be such a shock. When he was here a few weeks ago he seemed like the picture of health."

"He did, didn't he? I can hardly believe this. It's just beginning to sink in."

There was another knock on the door, and Cori opened it to see Jessalyn waiting to come in. She immediately hugged Cori, gently pulled her over to the sofa, and said, "Tell us everything." Jessalyn then realized she hadn't really greeted anyone, so she sat up straight and greeted Mrs. B. "I'm sorry, Mrs. B. Hello. Thank you so much for coming over so quickly. I didn't want Cori to be alone."

"I'm so glad you thought of me. I'm going to leave you two alone, and I'll check in with Cori tomorrow." She left quietly.

"I didn't mean to alarm you, Jessalyn."

"This is alarming. Tell me what you know."

"It's all my fault. I had this thought, no matter how fleeting it was, that he was doing too much. I traipsed him to Maine for Thanksgiving, and then all over Laurel Ledge and Hartford looking for information on his birth family. And the trips here from Arizona, all because of me. I can't imagine what it was like for him to find out a few weeks ago his mom had died of CF right after he was born, and his dad was severely depressed and committed suicide. Then he drove in the snow to the Adirondacks to meet his grandmother for the first time. Can you imagine the strain? I was so thoughtless to have him do all of this. But what did occur to me was that he shouldn't be playing with peds patients at the hospital. That's just not okay. The possibility of infection is enormous. You know that!"

"Cori, yes, I know that. Please don't blame yourself or Roman. Let's focus on a moment at a time."

"That's what Ainsleigh said she is doing."

"That's all we can do, isn't it? If we are going to talk about what's happened, we also must talk about how well Roman, Ainsleigh and you, mostly you, have made sure that he takes care of himself. The best predictor of his prognosis is how well he has kept his lungs clear over time. You all stay with the program without fail. There is a lot the hospital will do for him before making any decision on the health of his lungs. As much as we don't want to talk about it, a lung transplant is a good and viable answer, if he really needs it. I'll do a little more research, and we can talk about it at length. They aren't going to decide right away. Okay?"

"Yes. I'm sorry I flew off the handle."

"No worries, Cori. I'm willing to hear anything you have to say, but I worry if you're blaming yourself or wishing the last few weeks could be 'undone.'"

"Thanks."

"Are you in any mood to chat about something else."

"Yeah. What?" Cori stopped and gave her a clueless glance.

Jessalyn gave her a gentle shove. "What? What do you mean, what? You text me on the flight to Arizona that you're with THE "stranger!" You text me a few days later that he's in the next city and you've spent time with him? You send a final text that he's moving to Laurel Ledge! That's what!"

"Oh." Cori smiled despite the situation. "We had a wonderful time. Probably so wonderful that I overlooked the clues as to what might have been going on with Roman."

"Talk about the stranger."

"We sat together on the flight out west, so we had a long time to cover the 'get to know you' material. He's accepted the job of Executive Director at the recovery complex, you know, The Landing. We texted a lot while I was away, and we spent a part of a couple of days together. I tried not to wish for more since it was his last couple of weeks with his friends before moving here. He came east a few days ago."

"So, are you going to see each other?"

"I hope so. He's seems like such a good guy, and we had a good time together."

"You haven't told me his name."

"Oh. Yeah. Micah Flores."

"What's his background? Is he also in recovery?"

"You don't waste any time, do you?"

"Not usually."

"His experience came from his dad's addiction to alcohol. His dad couldn't deal with the compulsion and with his family at the same time. His dad's relationship with his family was destroyed because it was nil, and eventually the addiction destroyed him too."

"A couple of short sentences to describe a lifetime of destruction."

"Yeah. So, Micah has a degree in addictions counseling and an MBA. They're lucky to have him. He's also studying for a doctorate in Divinity. Besides running the center, he also will be preaching on Sundays and Wednesday evenings."

"You were going to volunteer at the center, right? Was it because of him?"

"Pure coincidence, if you believe in coincidences. I had attended a couple of Sunday services there and went through the orientation before I knew the "stranger" I had seen around town was interviewing there. I still didn't know his name or that he had the job until we were together on the plane or in line to board the plane."

"It's a great story, Cori. You really have a lot to look forward to. Stay with it. Roman and Ainsleigh will let you know when they need you, and they will need you. Stay strong for when the time comes."

"Good talk."

Chapter 3

Cori called Ainsleigh before leaving for work in the morning. The interventions seemed to be making Roman more comfortable, and Ainsleigh told Cori to call him and chat a little later in the day as time from work allowed.

Cori arrived at Amity Associates a little earlier than usual hoping for some extra time to get up to speed on the multitude of incoming assignments. She preferred cases requiring only email or teleconferencing until she knew more about Roman's situation. Travel was likely, though, since many cases involved the need for an on-site counselor either for the assistance of several employees or even consultation on the work environment.

She reported to Sophie Gaston before going to her desk. Often it was Sophie who triaged the cases and dispatched them to the counselors and consultants.

"Hey Sophie. How's it been?"

"Hi Cori. It's quiet right this moment. We were able to be at 'skeleton crew' so to speak for some of the holiday week. I just got back a couple of days ago, and it's been nonstop until this morning."

"Oh good." Cori joked. "Probably, you don't need me. I'll just go home."

"Wait, wait, wait. That's not what I mean! No, no, no, no, no."

"I tried. What's up?"

"I actually need you to travel."

"Oh. Okay. Solo or a team?"

"This one's solo, Cori. I can't tell from the intake information exactly what is going on. But it's at a prestigious small college, and I think it might be another case of harassment. The file has been shared with you. I think they want you to get on it right away."

Cori suspected the case called for a team despite Sophie's declaration that it was a solo assignment. She was willing to give pushback when she had a strong hunch about a case, but seldom put Sophie in the middle. Her plan was to make travel arrangements and spend some time researching the project. She needed to know why a male and a female weren't being dispatched.

North Carolina was a greater distance than she wanted to drive, so she arranged a flight out of Hartford later that evening. She opened the shared file and read the intake information. From what she could gather, an administrative assistant in the Department of English had collapsed and was taken to a local Emergency Department. Nothing medical seemed responsible, yet any mention of a discharge brought on an anxiety attack. She was transferred to the mental health unit, but all she would say about her work was that she couldn't go "back to that place."

The woman provided a release for the hospital to contact the college, but she became less anxious after an overnight stay and was released. Ultimately it was decided an outside agency should complete a site visit. Cori was impressed, in a way, by the college's response.

Byron Camp was the counselor with whom she teamed the most often. She decided to check his office to see if he was in. Though he was on paternity leave, she knew he still spent some time in the office.

"Hey Byron. How are Cheri and the baby?"

"Cori! At last! I think I'm here more than you are!" They were friends as well as co-workers and frequently took advantage of any instance where they could jokingly deride the other. "The girls are doing well. I think Cheri has successfully synced her schedule to sleep when the baby sleeps. Which is far more during the day than at night at this point. So, I help with the baby when I can, but mostly I try to keep the house running. I usually come in for a couple of hours during their morning nap!"

"It sounds like you have it figured out pretty well."

"Until we don't. Then we'll shift gears and deal with the fallout! It's all quite an adventure, and we're completely smitten with her. I don't think Cheri will be returning to full-time work anytime soon. That's why I keep showing up. If I don't, I'm afraid I'll get too attached to staying home."

"You may be sleep-deprived, but you look very content."

"I am. So, you need to get me caught up on your life, too. I got your texts and am wondering about this new interest in your life."

Cori told him a little about Micah, but she knew he would want to know about Roman as well. She thought she had a handle on her emotions, but she broke down as she was telling him.

Byron let her explain all the facts as she knew them as well as the guilt she felt over the physical and emotional strain that Roman had been through. He was stunned but tried to reassure her.

"Cori, for years you and your parents took daily care of Roman, sometimes involving hours of therapy. When they died, you were left to carry on until he was able to take over some of the coordination of services. Until he was married, you did nothing but focus on his health and your career.

"I understand how long you felt responsible for anything that happened to Roman, but it's not your responsibility anymore. Roman and Ainsleigh are responsible, and they do very well. No one should pressure anyone to feel guilty. They've done a great job. Have you spoken with Roman, by the way?"

"No. I'm about to call him."

"Go ahead. Let's talk again after you do."

"Uh, I actually came in about a case, too."

"Oh. What's up?"

"If I shared a file with you, would you give me your take on it?"

"Sure. I'll look at it while you call Roman."

Cori returned to her office, shared the file with Byron, and called Roman's cell. He answered on the first ring.

"Hi Cori." He didn't sound well at all.

"Hey Roman." She was fighting tears, and she knew he would recognize it in her voice. "I'm so sorry for how you feel. How are you today?"

"I know I sound sick. But I'm already much better than when I arrived at the hospital. They think it's an infection. It's serious, and it will take a lot to clear it up. Just pray. I think it's going to be okay."

"You're always so positive."

"Why not?"

"There it is. Thanks. I'll let you go. Rest."

"Yup. But I wanted to tell you that Helen is planning to move here."

Cori was taken aback, but she didn't want him to know. "Oh, how do you feel about it?"

"I think it's great. She'll live with us until an apartment is available at an assisted living franchise that is part of the same organization where she lives in the Adirondacks."

"Oh. Is Ainsleigh happy about it too?"

"Definitely."

"I sense that you're fading a bit. I really should let you go this time. Prayers for sure."

"Thanks, Sis."

Cori was shaken. She tried not to be hurt. They didn't need her, but they needed Helen, who was almost a stranger?

It was such an effort to focus on work after their chat, but she really needed to answer her messages. She took notes on them all, but the one from Claris Sullivan in the legal department piqued her interest. Claris had supported Cori through a difficult case involving the death of a high school student in Vermont just before the holidays. From the beginning, Cori suspected foul play, and together they garnered the interest of folks who exposed the coverup.

"Hi, Claris. It's Cori. It's good to hear from you, and you have my attention!"

"Thanks Cori. First, what about that guy you'd been spying on around town and ended up flying with to Arizona?"

"Quick answer, we got together a few times over the holidays. It was good. Really good. I hope we can continue where we left off."

"Nice. That's great to hear. How are Roman and Ainsleigh?"

"Roman's struggling with his health. I can't help but think he has worn himself out lately. They're even talking about a lung transplant."

"Oh, Cori. I'm so sorry. Are you going back?"

"That's a longer story but, no, not right now. I'll be sure to keep you posted on Roman. Now, are you going to tell me about your mysterious message?"

"I want to. Very much. But it's confidential and will take a bit of time to do it justice. Do you have time for dinner?"

"I actually have travel plans for Amity. Should I postpone?"

"No, no, no Cori. If you have time now, that's okay with me."

"Of course. Your place or mine?"

"I'd prefer not at Amity for now."

"Wh-What? Why?"

"I'll explain. How about meeting me at Trent's office in Hartford? I can text the address."

Cori was perplexed and wanted to ask more questions, but she trusted Claris as much as just about anyone in her life. "Sure, if that's what you need."

Cori couldn't come up with any ideas on what Claris had in mind nor why Trent would be involved. Trent Preston was a friend of Claris and, as an assistant district attorney, he had been integral in setting them up with the folks who prosecuted the case in Vermont.

Trent's office was on the ninth floor of a skyscraper in the capitol district. Had she known the difficulty parking would present, she would have pushed back a bit on the location.

She was buzzed in, and Claris was waiting for her there. She and Trent embraced. Cori's first instinct was to open with "what is this all about anyway." But she refrained and waited for their lead.

Claris broke the silence. "You're probably wondering why all of the cloak and dagger."

"Ya' think?"

Claris and Trent both smiled, and Claris continued. "We have tentatively agreed to join a task force that has the purpose of investigating, interdicting, and prosecuting cases of human trafficking. We need to have a counselor on the task force. You have the skills, credentials, and resilience that we need and would like you to consider joining us."

"Are you serious? Wait. Where-did-this-come-from? How did this all start? No. I don't know. I don't even know what to ask. Just talk. Tell me everything."

Trent broke in. "I was contacted by the Homeland Security a few weeks ago. They have tracked activity from New York City to Hartford and even Laurel Ledge, they think. This is very confidential, Cori. No matter what you decide, you can't say anything about this. They know Compass Points plays a role, they're just not sure how."

Compass Points again. The shelter for pregnant women in Laurel Ledge was the source of salacious rumors, but none had been substantiated as far as Cori knew.

"Cori, are you still with us?"

"I don't know. An understatement would be to say I am astonished. I know you're not kidding, but I still can't believe you're thinking about doing this. I don't understand why you would or why you think I would either. What could, or would, I possibly do?"

"We've worked with you, Cori. We know you see things that others don't or won't. You know how to expose facts and how to not be fooled by pat answers. You're not afraid of conferred power. In fact, you're highly suspicious of it! And you have a heart for true justice. Human slavery is one of worst affronts to human rights."

"Aren't you going to be in danger?"

"We're probably going to research legal interpretations, patterns of travel and commerce, seek warrants and such rather than be involved with the bad guys; but there is that possibility of danger."

"I don't even know if I have it in me to consider this but tell me everything you can. Are you leaving Amity, Claris? Is Trent leaving the prosecutor's office?"

"Our offices are involved. Amity has secured private donors and is setting up a foundation to help fund our part of the task force. Trent's office also is involved. We'll still be involved in occasional cases at Amity and the DA's office. Very few people will know how we're spending most of our time. We're going to be in Los Angeles to begin training."

"I think you both are amazing. This is incredible. I know I'm letting my pessimism about the enormity of the subject get in the way of my believing this is happening. I know you'll give me time to think about it, won't you?

"Of course. I know it would be hard to leave when you've just started a new relationship. If going to LA becomes the only roadblock, we'll find a way around that obstacle. That's how much we want you."

"Thank you. That, among many things, crossed my mind."

"We have one more request."

"Okay."

"Will you and a guest, read that Micah, join us for our wedding in a couple of weeks?"

"Wait, what? A wedding? A wedding? And in a couple of weeks? When did all of this happen?"

Claris and Trent looked at each other and grinned. Cori saw they both were blushing. She might have been blushing as well.

"We've been friends for a long time. You might be thinking it was the trip with you to Vermont that was the beginning of our becoming serious. If so, you are right."

Emphatically, Cori said, "I am so happy for you. More than I can say. This is the best news! It's perfect! I will be thrilled to attend your wedding. What day, when, what time?"

"The chapel at the Northfield Mount Hermon campus in Gill, Massachusetts. Trent's dad graduated from there. It's January break, so they gave us a special dispensation since it's available on the day we requested."

"My great-grandmother came from that area. The campus is beautiful and so is the chapel, though I've never been inside. It's going to be wonderful. This is so exciting."

Cori was sincere but rambling. She was distracted for a moment about another unsettled part of her life . . . another burning issue for which she wanted an explanation. Before the holidays and while they were pursuing Roman's family of origin, they happened to find documents indicating that Cori also was adopted. It was something she had never suspected. She was named Cora after her great-great-grandmother. Or the woman she thought was her great-great grandmother. Talking about that area of Massachusetts brought it back in full force. For now, she knew she had to return to the conversation.

"Yes. We're so excited."

"How can you split your focus between a wedding and getting involved in helping law enforcement interdict humans that are trafficked? This is surreal."

"It is for us, too."

"When do you leave for LA?"

"Soon after the wedding."

"What can I do to help . . . with the wedding? I can't even wrap my head around the task force yet."

"It has to be simple. The invitations are in the mail; yours should arrive soon, by the way. We chose an anonymous donation instead of favors, but you can know that it is the foundation for the task force. The flowers for the wedding party are ordered and will be delivered to the chapel, and the florist has agreed to decorate the chapel for us. There's a small tavern in town that is putting on a modest reception, and there's a cool bed and breakfast in a nearby town for anyone who wants lodging. We're not having a rehearsal, so no rehearsal dinner! This is a totally stripped-down version of a wedding!"

"The weather this time of year can be a challenge. Do you have a snow date?" Cori was half-kidding.

"We do. The restaurant is usually closed on a Sunday, so they're just going to hold everything for an additional day and open for us on Sunday if need be. The florist will pack the flowers so that they will survive for an additional day. If the snow can't be cleaned up in a day, then we're going to have to rethink the whole plan."

Cori needed to get back to the office. She apologized for having to run, but Trent and Claris simply asked her to be in touch with questions.

Claris made it even more direct. "The more you know about the task force, the more you'll realize you're perfect for the team."

Cori didn't feel complimented, though she should. News of the task force was just too unreal.

Chapter 4

Cori had been away from her desk so long that she suspected Byron would have left for home. She had just resumed routine responses to messages when he knocked on the jamb of her office door, which was open.

"Is everything okay, Cori?"

"Oh, ah, in a way. Roman thinks he has improved some. That it's an infection that may be hard but possible to treat."

"Yet, you're upset."

"Helen is moving out there."

"Helen?"

"His newly discovered grandmother."

"Oh, sorry. I had forgotten her name. She lives in upstate New York, right?"

"Yeah."

"This bothers you."

"Yeah. Some. I guess I'm confused. They really haven't gotten to know each other. She gave him up for adoption after her daughter passed away. She didn't want to care for another sick child."

"But she does now. If more people could know themselves that well, I think we'd have a safer world. It was fortunate for Roman that he had your family growing up, and she's ready to be the grandma he needs now."

"Byron, I just can't lose him."

"I know, Cori. I do." To distract her, and out of curiosity, he changed the subject abruptly. "Have you been in touch with Micah since you arrived back in town?"

"No."

"Cori. Why not? You need him."

"I'm afraid I'll scare him off with my problems. I don't know him that well or how he'll react."

"Don't you want to find out? Isn't that part of being in a relationship? He knows about Roman's health?"

"Yeah. Yes, he does."

"Call him. Spend a couple of hours with him before your flight. Promise?"

"Maybe."

"Do you want to know my take on the case you're taking on?"

"Oh, yes. Please."

"I think a team needs to address what's going on . . . eventually. I'd be willing to bet it's a "Me Too" situation. I judge it should be fine for you to make a quick visit to begin your support of whatever is going on with this woman and maybe to gather some information for a phase two."

"Yes. That makes sense."

"Are you going to be up to this?"

"Yes."

At that point a co-worker knocked quickly on the open door. "Hi. Sorry to interrupt. I just wanted to let you know, Cori, that someone came by to see you about an hour ago. You were out at the time. So, he left."

Cori was curious and hopeful about who that might have been. "Did you get a name?"

"No. It might sound cliched, but he was the quintessential 'tall, dark and handsome' type. I hope you find out who he was. He looked like he was worth it!"

Byron teased a bit. "Sound like Micah, maybe?"

"I think it does. I hope so."

"Call."

Chapter 5

Cori stared at her cell for several seconds before dialing. These decisions required a lot of thought. *Should I call his cell or his office? Will I mention that someone came by to see me? Can I do this without talking about Roman? If I talk about Roman, will I scare him off with my hysterics? Is this the best time to call? Do I dare ask him to get together?* Byron's order still sounded in her head. "Call."

She dialed his office and felt like a coward.

"Landing at Laurel Ledge. How may I help you?"

"May I please speak with Micah Flores?"

Identifying herself and the receipt of a pleasant request to "please hold" followed. Soon she was live with Micah.

"Hey. I came by to see you at Amity, but you were out."

Ice broken; major question answered. She relaxed a bit. "I'm sorry about not seeing you. I hope I haven't lost my chance."

They made plans to snow shoe through the town common later in the afternoon. It was his suggestion, and he supplied the snowshoes courtesy of the Landing's equipment closet. She skipped lunch to process some of the backlog of work waiting for her.

The conditions were icy, and they slipped more than they walked. Though usually competent on snow shoes, the conditions got to her, and eventually she fell and pulled Micah with her. They laughed. He helped her to her feet and held hands as she tried again. After trudging the length of the common and back, they decided to walk to the Sandwich Club for a cup of coffee—sans the snowshoes.

Walking arm in arm was far more than the comfort provided by the warmth of his body, it was the obvious excitement of being close to him. As much as she loved coffee, she didn't want to let go when they arrived at their destination.

They sat side by side with their steaming cups of coffee and a frosted lemon scone to share. He moved close to her, stroked her hand and softly spoke. "I've missed you. You probably guessed that when you found out I was stalking you at your office."

She laughed. She hadn't expected this unvarnished expression of interest in her, and she felt an uncharacteristic freedom to enjoy his attention and display her attraction to him. He broke off the first piece of scone and fed it to her. While she was savoring her morsel, he broke off a huge piece for himself. They laughed because of the discrepancy in the portions, but mostly because they were happy to be together.

"Let's have dinner tomorrow night. I'm just getting acquainted with some of the fine dining in the region, and I wondered what your personal favorite is?"

"I would love to, but I have to go out of town tonight on a consulting case. I only plan to be away one night, but it could be pretty late when I return."

"A late dinner will work. Do you mind talking about your assignments?"

"I don't mind. I can anticipate we both deal with confidential information, but otherwise I'm willing to discuss what I can. All I really know is that I'll be assisting an employee of a small liberal arts college who is upset enough to avoid returning to work. I think it will be a continuing project, and my initial visit will give me insight on how to help in the long run. How about I call you when I get back?"

"I can't wait. When do you leave?"

"In a few hours. I really need to go home, load my suitcase, and get to the airport. I just wanted to see you before leaving again." It felt good to admit it.

"Here's a suggestion. Let me drive you to the airport. I can pick you up when you return, and if the timing is right, we can have the promised dinner in Hartford."

She did the normal interrogation about whether it really was a good plan for him, and with enthusiastic reassurances, she agreed.

As she packed, she couldn't help but be proud that she hadn't vented with him about Roman's situation. *I can't hide it from him, though. If I do, he'll question my willingness to confide in him when he finds out. Maybe on the trip to airport.*

The occasion to tell him about Roman's hospitalization did come up in the car, and immediately she felt better. He spoke and interrupted her thoughts.

"I'm sorry if you didn't think you could tell me right away about Roman."

"It wasn't about you, Micah. It was about me. I needed some distance from it and some closeness to you. I know they're not mutually exclusive, but at the time, it was just what I needed."

"Then okay."

They really didn't want to separate, but Cori was not on the earlier side of check-in. They hugged, and she was a little surprised when he kissed her good-bye. She looked into his eyes and smiled. He smiled and rolled his eyes a bit and defended himself.

"I know it's not the best setting for a first kiss, but I just didn't want to wait any longer."

"Then okay," echoing his good-natured response.

She squeezed his hand, turned, and proceeded to float through the line.

Chapter 6

The campus of Colton College was lovely, but Cori's first impression was a bit cynical. Despite GPS-friendly addresses and online research about campus parking lots and building locations, it was frustrating to find her way to Armstrong Hall, which housed the College of Arts and Sciences. The signage was terrible. The country club mantra seemed to fit as far as Cori was concerned. "If you don't know, you don't belong here."

As she trudged through campus she was sensitive to more of the stifling aspects of the milieu. She was having flashbacks to her university days where she observed blue collar employees, whether landscapers, carpenters or custodians, who were invisible to the students and professors. They performed their duties as if in another dimension.

Administrative staff interacted freely with the non-student, non-professorial community. They were the ones who

interpreted the physical needs of the campus to the skilled individuals who ultimately would keep the apparatus functioning.

What was not lacking in signage was the boasting about diversity and acceptance prevalent in the life of the campus. *These
people are ensconced in their own self-absorbed, narrow-minded
spectrum that belies every scintilla of love, tolerance and acceptance
to which they lay sole claim.*

Her meeting with the Dean of the College of Arts and Sciences
revealed nothing helpful. He feigned cluelessness about any in-
sights on the situation that brought her to campus. She found
him dismissive and sophomoric. Undoubtedly a giant in his field,
he possessed nothing in skills beyond the rarified environment
he inherited and perpetrated on recurring generations of willing candidates duly obligated to understand what is required to
receive from and feed back to their instructors in order to earn
the credentials that will show the world they are worthy of conferred elite status in society.

Yes. I am cynical of a place like this.

Her next stop was the home of the individual she was hired to
counsel. Lorena had been released from the hospital, but whether her release was based on actual health, or simply that she was
timed-out under managed care, was not clear to Cori.

She rang the doorbell, and the door was answered by a young,
attractive woman.

"I'm Cori Sellers from Amity Associates. I'm here to see
Lorena."

"I'm Lorena. It's nice to meet you." She held out her hand,
shook Cori's, and invited her in. *She's very poised and courteous.*

Lorena spoke first after offering Cori a seat and some coffee, both of which were accepted. "I'm not sure how this goes or what is expected of me."

Cori outlined the information typically shared about confidentiality, and then offered assurances to Lorena that she was free to define their time together in any way she wished. "I have no goals of my own, Lorena. This can be about anything that will assist you."

"I don't want to be rude, but aren't you hired by the college?"

"My firm is hired by the college, yes. I'm here to help you. My only concern about the college is if something detrimental is systemic to the college. That is why an outside agency is needed."

"Is the client always right in your eyes?"

"No one is always right!" They both laughed. "It's not about choosing sides, per se. It's about listening to you and carving out what's important, fair, doable, maybe? Those are my words. Let's hear some of your words."

"It's really simple. The College is the only game in this town. It's where we plan to have our careers, at least for those of us who aren't going to college . . . right away that is. I'm working with an impossible supervisor. She is such a phony. That's not exactly right. She really can do good work. But she doesn't. She does everything in her power to make it look as though any inferior work is mine and any of my good work is due to her or someone else. She's a master at it.

"I had a cruise scheduled months in advance and the time off had been approved. I had proof of it. But her copy of the approval miraculously disappeared, and she convinced human resources, who had a copy, that it would create an undue hardship for me to be gone during the scheduled time since she hadn't had time to plan around it. So, she simply couldn't approve a last-minute request as much as she wanted to.

"So much of what she does is so devious that I can't even begin to explain it or how she gets away with it. Of course, any other job I apply for, she ruins my chances. I don't list her as a reference, but they call her anyway. Even though that's not an acceptable practice, I can't prove what's going on.

"If I try to take a break or go to the bathroom, I have to go by her desk. She questions me every time, and if I continue, she goes directly into the Dean's office and closes the door.

"Everyone thinks I was hospitalized in mental health because I am crazy. That's not the way it happened. I found out later my supervisor knows one of the nurses in the Emergency Department who has been there the longest.

"I think I just want to get out of town."

Cori took advantage of the break. "I don't blame you. Is that a possibility and would you do that?"

"If I could. My parents are back and forth. They said they would help me get started somewhere else. But I know they would be sacrificing a lot. I think they wish this could be made right. I would too, but that is way naïve."

"I want to make sure of something, and it's quite personal."

"Go ahead."

"Is there any sexual impropriety going on?"

Lorena snorted. "No doubt. I think some of the staff are so gaga over the professors and all that power and knowledge . . . and money. They would count it a privilege to sleep with some of the attractive faculty. To them it's seems like instant status.

No one is pressuring me that way, though. I am glad about that at least."

No one said anything for a moment. Lorena broke the silence.

"Do you have any ideas?"

"I do, but they're really unorthodox."

"It won't hurt to say what they are."

"I will. Very soon. First, I want to rule out anything medical. Can we get your records from the ED and the behavioral health unit?"

"I have a copy here.

"Do you mind if I read through?"

"No. It's fine. It's past time for lunch. Could I offer you a sandwich?"

"That would be lovely, if you don't mind."

"I make my own aioli for chicken salad. Would that be okay?"

"You bet."

Lorena returned, and Cori had the gist of the reports by then. They took a break to enjoy their chicken salad on croissants.

"I noticed something in the ED summary that could explain your symptoms."

"Really. What?"

"You were dehydrated. This stands in contrast to the volume produced when they asked you to void for a specimen. When you add the stress factor to either of these, it can cause fainting. Do you know what was going on?"

"I hadn't taken a break for anything that day. I had it with her bullying. I apologize for using that word. It's so overused. It feels like it fits."

"You're right. People love the buzzword, 'bully.' That's what this woman is, though. I think there should be a stronger word for when it rises to the level of jeopardizing employment, safety, or even breaking a law. You could have a lawsuit. I will address this for you in my report. I assume the hostility of the ED nurse kept her from telling you the medical reason for the symptoms.

"That said, one of the most inventive methods I've encountered for dealing with bullies is to joke, cajole, and agree with them to a certain extent. For example, if she belittles someone's work in public, the injured party simply jokes saying, 'You would think I could do a lot better with the ace trainer I have!' It brings her into the circle of responsibility. Bystanders are more apt to become neutral. That's a good thing. If the audience is neutralized and the target is taken off the bull's-eye, there is no more point to the belittling.

"It takes wit, patience, and a real sense of humor. The target must stop thinking or acting like a victim. Every effort is aimed at bringing the responsibility back to your supervisor. It won't be possible in every situation.

"Whenever you can, talk her up to whoever will listen, including her. Be very public about announcing to her that it's time for a break. It might be embarrassing to announce your bathroom breaks, but I recommend it, and it's going to be part of my report.

"I don't intend to leave you alone in this. I will document it for the Dean and for your supervisor. I notice her name is Helena. I suppose when we're trying to combat bullying, I shouldn't encourage name-calling. But I was imagining a few epithets she could have reaped over the years."

"I plead the fifth!"

"Good choice!"

"I have some recommendations. I have a curriculum for coaching on some of these techniques. I would like to set up at least weekly sessions for role-playing imaginary scenarios and for debriefing actual incidents.

"You don't have to commit to anything right now. Call me with what you'd like to do. In the meantime, start a blog. Don't name names or even say it comes from experiences on a job. Speak in terms of adages and generalities. Write a few before you publish. If you allow advertising, you could make a little money."

"I like it. Really, I do. Let's make it happen."

"I want to emphasize, it's not easy."

"It hasn't been easy."

"I know. I'll see the Dean, and I'll be in touch."

"Thanks."

Cori stopped by the student center and typed up her report. She contacted the Dean, and he agreed to see her again. Cori shared the new medical information and gave a quick summary of the report, which was what she and Lorena had discussed. She followed up by documenting her conversation with the Dean, printing both reports in one of the student computer labs, and having the Dean sign the whole package. She gave copies to the Dean's assistant for the file and took a copy to human resources. She asked them to share a copy with Lorena's supervisor. If Helena had a rebuttal, Cori indicated she would be happy to return and talk with her as well.

Despite her jaded view of the campus polity, their trumpeted egalitarian accomplishments made them susceptible to documented criticism about differential treatment. Every social group had its Helena, it seemed. "*As common as muck.*" Or as her dad would say, 'horse manure.' She wasn't sure why that saying she heard from her dad popped into her mind. As a youngster, she wrongly sensed it referred to a day when horse-drawn carriages were the primary mode of transportation and thus a statement on how plentiful the detritus was. It brought about an absurd musing about what it would have been like if horse owners, like dog owners, were required to carry bags to pick up the animal's refuse.

It was late when she left campus. She had been updating Micah with texts, so he wasn't shocked when she called to let him know that dinner wouldn't be possible.

"I am disappointed, though." He texted back.

"So am I. I'm afraid my life can be like this all too frequently."

"You haven't seen it yet, but so can mine. The best thing we can do is have as much understanding for each other as we wish for ourselves. Does that make any sense?"

"Of course."

"It would feel better if you waited until tomorrow to fly home."

"I was thinking the same thing."

"Text me later about your flight? I'll pick you up if I possibly can. If not, I'll have someone from my staff available."

"Will do. I hope it's you. I'm looking forward to seeing you again."

"You can't wait for the hello kiss!"

She was glad he couldn't see her blush, and she was equally glad that he had said it. "Miss you."

"Miss you too."

Chapter 7

Cori admitted to herself how good it was to think about things other than Roman. Work was compelling her to problem solve once again, and her near obsession with Micah was all encompassing and a feeling she had never had before—at least not in recent memory.

In fact, she hadn't checked on Roman since before she left Laurel Ledge. Even though the hour was late, she decided to call.

"Hello." Roman's answer was flat.

"Hi. Is everything okay?"

"Should I ask you that?"

"I'm sorry I haven't been in touch. I got a little caught up in the current case."

"It seems like an opposite reaction from what I would expect after talking to Byron."

"Byron! What on earth is going on?"

"I couldn't reach you on your cell, so I called Amity. Byron happened to be there, so the person who answered the telephone said he might know if you could be reached at your work site. I was surprised by what he told me."

"Which was . . ."

"He said you resent Helen's involvement and are distrustful of her commitment to helping Ainsleigh and me."

Cori was astounded. Never would she have imagined a conversation between Byron and Roman. *Why would Byron cast her fears in such a negative light and to the person who could be hurt by them the most?* She was so stunned that she made no attempt to provide a context or explanation.

"I care about Helen and you very much. I am glad she will be in your life. I'm sorry if I hurt any of you. I don't think I can talk about this any further right now. Are you feeling okay?"

"I am."

"Good. We'll talk later."

"Yes. Later."

It was clear that if she experienced any moments of hope and pleasure, they were sure to be dashed to smithereens.

She didn't sleep that night. Instead, she tossed, turned, and wondered how she found herself in this situation and whether she had the energy to sort it out. But right now, she was angry.

Micah was able pick her up at the airport, and the promised kiss was there too. It was bold, as if they had been greeting each other this way on a routine basis. It was gentle as well. They lingered, and Cori loved everything about being close to him. He smelled so good, and the fragrance was familiar. Happy? Despite her lack of sleep and the added turmoil in her life, she was happy. His arms were muscular, and she felt safe. She took credit and pleasure as the depth of his breathing increased. Eventually he gave a gentle squeeze and reluctantly released his caress. He didn't stop looking at her, and she smirked at him.

He cocked his head a bit and gently asked, "What?"

"Oh, I'm just a little surprised that you are willing to kiss me in public--twice."

"I can't help myself!"

"Doesn't a 'pastor' have a public image to burnish?"

He bowed his body slightly and chuckled. "I guess I haven't really embraced that part of my job description. I'd rather embrace you! Do you have checked luggage?"

"Yes. It's probably the only bag left on the conveyor at this point!"

Micah finally interjected a question into the constant chatter on the drive to Laurel Ledge. "I sense a sleepless night in your recent past."

"Does it show?"

"Something about the eyes and the attempts to keep from yawning."

Cori inhaled deeply. *How much should I say? The more I say, the more trouble I heap on myself.* "I'm in trouble with my brother. It's my mouth again."

"Roman? The way you speak about him, I was under the impression there weren't the usual bumps in the road between you two."

"This is one of the first I can remember."

"How serious?"

"Enough."

"Let's talk more about this tonight. I have a speaking engagement for lunch followed by a staff training. How is an early dinner?"

"I'd like that."

Chapter 8

Cori was back at Amity after a quick lunch at her condo. It was a refuge in her current frame of mind. She went into action as she added a cover sheet to the report she had prepared for the Dean. Once again, she escaped having to follow the new procedures required by the Diagnostic Statistical Manual V (DSM V), which was used to diagnose clients in need of therapy or referrals for medication. It wasn't necessary for Lorena since behavioral health had addressed her anxiety. She simply turned them in to her supervisor, Blake Whitaker, and submitted her billable hours to date to accounting and gave her travel forms to Sophie Gaston.

* * *

What in the world am I going to do with the information about the task force? She and Micah had the "job-related confidentiality" talk, but she needed to talk about this. If they were married, they could talk about it under the guise of "pillow talk." *Isn't that how married couples rationalized breaking confidences?* Yet, she knew she couldn't talk about it. Not with Micah, not with anyone.

When they met at the restaurant, their pleasure in seeing each other was only expressed through a caress. Cori loved his touch and the sense of belonging. The restaurant was lively and noisy. Obviously observing their delight with each other, the maître de found a table for them away from the thick of the crowd.

They weren't interested in the food but managed to act as though it was at least a partial reason for being there. They chatted about a host of subjects. It was all about interacting--neither cared about the topic. Eventually a discussion of Sunday's activities was broached by Micah, and he asked if she would like to visit the service at the Landing.

"When I'm in town, that's where I've been attending."

"Oh. I thought you just volunteered there."

"Truth be told, I've spent more time there on Sundays than I have volunteering. It just hasn't come together yet."

"So, how did you come to attend services at the Landing?"

"A friend recommended it."

"Do you have your own home church?"

"I did."

"Uh huh."

"Yeah."

"Where? Did something happen?"

"Here. In Laurel Ledge. Ever since I can remember. Some folks were out to get me, so I left."

"Who? Why?"

"My former best friend, the pastor, the head of communication."

"I'm having trouble understanding . . ."

"Me too."

"What *do* you know?"

"The head of communication lodged a complaint about me, and they removed me from my role as leader with the elementary-aged youth group. My sense is my former best friend, Simone, used the trumped-up complaint to impress a powerful woman in the community who wanted me discredited. Simone is the director of youth programs there, so she was my boss as well as my friend. It's an average-sized church, and she wants to work for a mega church. This woman, Lourdes Dallas, can help her with that. From what I hear, it's in the works or even a done deal."

"That's not how a church works. Did you do anything to defend yourself against the charges or apologize in any way?"

"I wrote apologies with no result. Simone wouldn't talk about it. Roman and I met with the Pastor, but it wasn't at all productive. He was caught up in the momentum and had no skills to stop the train wreck."

"What did this Lourdes have against you?"

"Are you sure you want to hear this?"

"Of course." He was gentle, but emphatic.

"I am friends with a single mom and her little girl, whom I met through the youth group. Reina and Della Carbone are their names. Reina had been a resident at Compass Points years ago and subsequently lost her baby because she had been so badly beaten by her husband. Eventually she was found to be pregnant again and was hustled out of town.

"A few people had told me rumors, unproven, about a doctor at Compass Points. It involves inappropriate behaviors with the residents. He happens to be Lourdes' husband."

Micah noticed she was now hesitating. He encouraged her, "I'm with you so far."

"The only way this made sense was if Lourdes suspected Dr. Dallas was Della's dad. I finally was brave enough to ask Reina. She graciously told me the whole story. Her ex had found her and attacked her when she left Compass Points for a few hours of job hunting. She escaped from him, but that is how Della was conceived.

"A private detective helped Reina to relocate, courtesy of an unknown benefactor. I happened to know a private detective who worked for Lourdes because he had tried to seduce me on a business trip . . . also prompted by Lourdes. I confronted him and told him he owed me the whole story given what happened. He confirmed Lourdes had funded Reina's relocation. I asked if she suspected Della was Dr. Dallas's daughter. He couldn't confirm what she thought, but he had worked for her several times and it always appeared to be about suspected infidelities of her husband. I told him the truth about Reina and insisted that he promise to convince Lourdes of the truth. A few hours later it dawned on me that there's more to it than that."

"More than that. Really? Like what?"

"I'm adopted. I just found out a couple of months ago when we opened the court documents about Roman's adoption. When I tried to pursue the facts of my own adoption, I was shut down. The facts are never to be divulged. I suspect one of my parents is either Dr. Dallas or Lourdes."

He took her hand. "You have a lot of reason for distrust. I think I'm a little lost about the last part, though."

"My problems with Simone started at about the same time as my relationship with Della. That was my only hunch for a long time. Then, Roman told me about his inquiry, at about that same time, to Lourdes's legal firm. Did I tell you she's a lawyer? He contacted them about a document we were never meant to see involving an adoption a decade before his. Just about the time I was born, in fact. I think his inquiry about the document 'poked the bear.' He really was looking for clues about his own adoption."

There was a long silence. The only movement besides shallow breathing was Micah cupping her hands in both of his. He stared at their hands as if embarrassed that he could come up with no other way of showing support.

They were aware that the wait staff had been hovering—perhaps for some time. Some of the lights of the restaurant were dimmed, and most of the other patrons had left. They quickly paid the check and walked out into the biting cold, arm in arm. They hadn't said a word.

Having arrived in separate cars, their only opportunity to talk further would be in the cold. Micah spoke first.

"Cori, I have to be out of town for the next couple of days. I'll be in touch by texting and calling. I don't know what to say right now about all of this except I will do anything in my power to help. I don't know what that entails, but I trust you do or you will."

There was a crick in her voice as she said, "Thanks."

He kissed her, gently, but for a long time. She kissed back. The feeling was so wonderful that all stress and worry evaporated.

Chapter 9

Cori placed her morning call to Roman, who was doing better than anyone had expected. There were times when he was out of bed, and there was talk of sending him home with skilled nursing care. His conversations with Cori were cordial, which given their former bond, was stilted. They both were hurt, and it was perplexing to them why they couldn't help each other sort out the hurt and make it better.

She wanted to arrive early at the Landing in case she could see Micah before the service. A good-sized crowd already had gathered, and she was surprised to see that Reina and Della were there. She made her way to them, and they hugged as they expressed their surprise and delight in seeing each other.

"I didn't know you attended here." Cori was the first to speak.

"We haven't before. We heard there was someone new as the director of the Landing who also is serving as the Pastor, so we decided to visit. How about you, Cori?"

"I've been attending whenever I'm in town, which isn't a lot. The director is a new friend of mine."

"Friend as in just friends or special friend?"

"It seems special."

Reina reacted with a quiet but excited cheer. "Yay! That's so cool."

Della had been quiet but had a coy look on her face that was not lost on Cori.

"Don't worry Della. We're still going to have our girls' nights out. In fact, when are you free?"

"Anytime, but I don't want to cramp your style!"

Cori gave her a one-arm squeeze. "How do young people get so wise?"

"You don't know the half of it!" Reina acknowledged that Della was quite a match for her.

The time had passed quickly as they chatted, and they realized the songs were beginning. Cori felt at home immediately as they took their seats. The simplicity of the service was renewing. Micah spoke on the ancient text about Abram and Sarah leaving Haran and going to Canaan. When famine came, they went down to Egypt. Because of Sarah's beauty, Abram was convinced that they would kill him to get him out of the picture, and the authorities could take Sarah. In his dire fear for his life, he asked Sarah to lie and say she was his sister.

Cori thought Micah accurately identified Abram's mistakes, provided relevant conclusions for contemporary living and emphasized the mercy of God revealed through human weaknesses. Overall, it was a great reminder about shortcutting on matters of morality.

She stood in line, like everyone else, to be greeted by Micah with Reina and Della. She introduced them to Micah, and he asked if they had lunch plans. Reina insisted that she wasn't going to intrude on them, but Cori and Micah prevailed.

Cori made an almost daily appearance at the Sandwich Club, but this was only her second time since returning from Arizona. The time flew by, and Reina jumped up when she realized it was time for them to take Della to a special play date at a friend's house.

Micah and Cori stayed for coffee and dessert.

"You are gifted at speaking, Micah. That was excellent."

"Thank you."

"Do you get nervous?"

"Well, yeah. I can identify with a certain amount of stress. It helps in a way to stay focused."

"There's something in that passage that no one ever mentions."

"Uh oh. Has our relationship progressed to the level of sermon critiques at Sunday dinner?"

Cori knew he was joking. So, she gave it back. "That's the only reason I'm seeing you!"

He laughed. "Okay. Go ahead."

"Well, you were spot on in emphasizing Abram's lack of faith and rush to save his own skin. You also mentioned there was a definite impact on Sarah. You didn't use the words moral depravity, but it was clear that the culture of Egypt was so corrupt that Abram should never had ventured there just because times were tough. And, what they planned to do with Sarah was clearly human trafficking."

"I guess that was implicit, though I didn't use those words."

"Yeah. The emphasis usually seems to be on Abram's lie, or half-truth since Sarah was his half-sister, then on God's graciousness in forgiving Abram and honoring his covenant with him. But the enormity of this act is horrifying. That God would be gracious in preventing harm to Sarah is amazing also."

"I think that's clear as well. You care a lot about this."

"I do. I hope I haven't offended you."

She also hoped she hadn't tipped her hand about what was on her mind.

Chapter 10

The drive to Massachusetts for the wedding provided Micah and Cori with sought-after time to talk. They had spent time together whenever they could eke out a couple of mutual hours in their busy days. It was never enough.

Micah was dashing in his dark suit, and Cori reveled in the excitement of being close to him. She could tell the feeling was mutual and was glad she combined style with practicality. She wore a dress that was called a satin cocktail dress, but Cori chose it for a couple of features, mainly the asymmetric bateau neckline and ruching at the sides. It was longer than most cocktail dresses but still very flattering for her figure. She paired it with a faux fur bolero jacket that was low cut in the neck to one large button for fastening. The neckline of her dress was visible, and she was confident she wouldn't be cold. Though mesmerized by the appearance of the other, they did manage some conversation.

"Did you have a chance to talk to Roman today?"

"Uh huh. He's home and they're managing with daily nursing care. He's even spending time outside. They're keeping him on the transplant list. None of his doctors are sure that his lungs are in it for the long haul."

"Did the chat go well?"

"It's okay. He's way too sweet to be hostile to me. I have no idea if things ever will be the same between us, though."

"I don't know the answer, but I think you'll both find a way. I've been thinking about you and Simone, too."

"What? Why?"

"She was a good friend. Granted, it appears she let herself become a pawn in someone else's scheme, but I think reconciling a meaningful relationship is always a good idea. And the church, too."

"I tried. I can't get past the hurt."

"That's just it. You're still feeling hurt. That has to be resolved."

"You said it yourself, that's not how a church operates."

"They were duped, obviously. I was thinking, what if you were one of your clients? What would you say?"

"I'd coach them through it."

"Exactly. I can't do that the way you can, but I hope you'll give it some thought."

"As if I haven't already. Sorry. Okay. I'll give it some thought . . .along with everything else." The latter part was said under her breath, but he heard her.

"What 'everything else'?"

"Oh, you know. Roman, Byron, adoption."

"Yeah. It is a lot."

She almost tipped her hand once again. It wasn't subliminal. She wanted to talk to him about the plans of Trent and Claris in the worst way. Especially today since the day was all about them. Soon after their honeymoon, the task force would be pulled together. They would need her decision.

They arrived on the Mt. Hermon campus in the town of Gill about an hour before the ceremony. Cori wished she could conjure up the courage to explore Rustic Ridge. The narrow dirt road, along with the steep inclines and dangerous ledges were too much in winter weather. In summer weather, she loved seeing the cottages and reflecting on their history. Built by folks attending D.L. Moody's Summer Bible Conferences, some of the cottages were passed from generation to generation. Cori reminisced to Micah, "My mom loved to talk about Northfield and its history as is related to Moody. The summer conferences made Northfield into a famous summer resort during the late nineteenth and early twentieth centuries. A rich entrepreneur built a summer home fashioned after a French chateau near the Northfield campus, which had ninety-nine rooms and many turrets. Mom toured the chateau before it was torn down in the late sixties. I can't image why treasures like that can fall into disrepair."

They enjoyed the drive through part of the Northfield campus, with its Romanesque Revival buildings and the view of the mountains and vales in this beautiful part of the Pioneer Valley. The campus no longer belonged to the prestigious private school. Cori continued to interpret their tour.

"Many of the buildings are now owned and will be operated as a satellite campus of a private college. Claris spent a week here working with other volunteers and paid contractors, whose intent was to refurbish as much of the campus as possible for the opening of the Great Books College to be operated by the C. S. Lewis foundation. In the end, not enough money was raised, and the buildings once again went on the market. I know Claris was disappointed at the time. She must be thrilled that Trent had an alum connect that opened the door to the Gill campus as her wedding venue."

They agreed a return visit in the summer would be in order as they headed back to the Gill campus for the ceremony. The granite chapel was impressive with its medieval exterior architecture. Inside, bunches of willow branches painted white and sprinkled with glass glitter festooned each row of seating. The addition of sparkling lights on each gave the impression of a winter wonderland. Two larger white, lighted branches that were closer in size to a small tree surrounded the wedding altar. The arrangements perfectly accented and illuminated the dark interior of this stone architecture. *So much for simplicity.*

Cori caught her breath as Claris glided down the aisle. The attendants, Claris's older sister and her nieces, were given free rein to choose their dresses, and they were stunning despite the lack of style coordination. The colors were beautiful hues of red, and the style ranges were strapless, shoulders-only exposed, and long-sleeved; taffeta, organza, and velvet; tea length, cocktail length, and floor length.

On a typical day of work, Claris donned the choice of what many modern women referred to as a work uniform. Her preference was an off-white tie blouse with dark slacks or a skirt. She had varying length dark jackets as well. The image was something along the lines of the lead character on the television show, Madam Secretary.

Always tasteful, Claris now was revealing a more dramatic and daring side to her fashion proclivities. Her wedding dress was far from a uniformed selection. She was a vision in her silvery satin dress with beaded crystal straps, draped directional bodice and flared court-length train. Matching beaded crystal accented the gathers at her left hip. As she passed Cori and Micah and continued toward her love at the altar, the sexy corseted dress back added an even greater wow factor. The dress adorned her perfectly sculpted slim figure and the shimmering silver popped against the sparkling lights and snow-white branches.

Trent didn't hide his delight in this vision approaching him. His eyes were glistening, but he didn't shed a tear. It was clear that no one else existed in the cavernous sanctuary save his lovely bride. He sustained his attention to her and her alone throughout the ceremony.

Cori loved weddings, and this one was fabulous. She admitted to very few how much she dreaded receptions. To her, they were just boring. The waiting around, the assigned seating to show how important (or not) one was to the bride's family, the lousy food, the population of primarily women dancing together because men were unwilling to partner, all grated on her. Claris didn't know Cori's biases, but it was as though she did everything in her power to countermand Cori's preconceptions.

Claris and Trent arrived at the reception almost simultaneously with the guests. The photographer had to be very creative in capturing pictures with a minimum of poses. The food, which was delectable, was served immediately, and they proceeded to the cake cutting soon after everyone was served. Claris and Trent didn't smash cake in each other's faces nor down each other's gullets, and they took cake to each of their guests and greeted them all individually. Soon after, they said good-bye and they were off on their wedding trip.

There was music if their guests wanted to dance or a bar if they wanted to drink on their own dimes, or both. Guests also were free to move on with their lives with no guilt. Cori and Micah enjoyed a few dances together and left for Laurel Ledge.

"Did you enjoy the wedding?" Micah broke a long silence as they drove home.

"Oh, I did. It was a privilege to be part of something so beautiful. I loved how quickly everything moved along."

"You're all about brevity."

"I suppose. Is that a bad thing?"

"Not necessarily. When it comes to weddings, I agree. I can see why the bride and groom would want to move things along, if you know what I mean. None of what we saw was the main event."

Cori smirked—and blushed.

Chapter 11

It was Sophie Gaston's ringtone that sounded just before Cori left for worship on Sunday. "Hey Sophie. What's up?"

"I have a strange one, Cori."

"Hmm. Stranger than most, or ever?"

"Well, let's say most."

"Okay. Let's have it."

"A friend of Seavers's in the accounting department is working with a team of engineers and what not on a contract in Xi'an, China, on renewable building materials. That's why the attention to a case on a weekend. They're having trouble keeping the team going. So many leave before they are up to speed. With the lack of progress, the contract is in jeopardy. They want support right away. Seavers thinks they need an accountant, an investigator, and a counselor. So, that's what we're going to do."

"Would I leave right away?"

"As soon as possible. Someone from travel will make the arrangements if you decide to go. But we only have the cultural trainer at 3:00 this afternoon. I'm sorry that it doesn't give you much time to decide or prepare."

"I'll let you know by noon."

"Thanks. Talk to you then."

"Ah, Sophie. I have an immediate suggestion. Shouldn't someone interview the staff members who have left the team?"

"Absolutely. An investigator is already on it."

I don't know whether to be excited or frightened. I think this is the answer I've been waiting for though. I suspect the task force assignment is not what I want. This is what I should do.

It wouldn't do any good to text Micah right now since the service would be underway. She called Roman instead.

His voice sounded sleepy. "Hey Sis. Is everything okay?"

"Sorry if you were asleep."

"I sleep quite a bit. No need for an apology. Usually you're at the Landing by now."

"Right. I was about to leave when I got a call from work. They have an assignment in China for me."

"China. And just what does China need from you?"

"Thanks a lot! It's a team of U.S. engineer-types consulting on renewable building materials and energy distribution. They may need some help keeping up the morale of the team, I guess. I just wanted you to know and make sure you think it's okay for me to be out of the country."

"Of course. Live your life; do your job. If it's what you want to do. Is it?"

"I think so."

"What about Micah? I've been under the impression you've been quite infatuated with each other. Do you want to leave him right now?"

"I really don't. I can't keep this job and not travel, though. Luckily, it's the same for Micah and his job, so he understands. We'll have to build a relationship that can thrive under the circumstances. I don't want to think of any alternatives!"

"Good attitude."

"I hate being out of touch with what's happening with you too."

"We've got this."

"Okay. I'll let you know when I've made my final decision."

"Stay safe. This is a big deal."

"Yes. I suppose it is."

By then she knew it was safe to text Micah. "I might have an overseas assignment right away. Would like to talk about it with you."

He texted back right away. "What's good for you? I have a meeting at 7:00 this evening."

She was disappointed. That would have been a good time to have dinner and would fit the best into her schedule as well. "I can be free by 5:00 or so."

"That works. Where?"

"Where else?"

"Sandwich Club it is!"

There were more folks at Amity than on a typical Sunday. She hadn't checked her emails or her voicemails all weekend, so she spent time on them. She texted Sophie that she was planning on going and would let her know for certain by 7:00 that evening. It was nearly time to join the orientation meeting on hot topics of concern when traveling and working in China when Byron popped into her office. She hadn't seen him since she vented to him about her concern for Roman after which he betrayed her confidence.

"Hi Cori. I've checked your office the few times I've been in, but I haven't been able to catch you."

"Oh. Is there something I can do for you?"

"No. Just wanted to see how things are going."

"Well, Roman and I managed to talk after what you told him. But it just isn't the same."

"Cori."

"No. Byron. What were you thinking? Do you know how hurt he was and I am?"

"You need to listen. I don't think you were seeing how right the time is for you to step away. It wasn't fair to be jealous of Helen or to blame her or think she was taking your place or whatever it was that you were thinking."

"I was upset. I don't even know what I was thinking . . . especially about why I would confide in a friend."

"You don't know the context. Look, Cori, Roman and Ainsleigh need their space. If they won't tell you, I will. And you need your space too. You're not the caregiver anymore. Stop feeling responsible."

"Roman said that? They need their space?"

"He said that."

She closed her eyes as if she couldn't take in what he had said, and then opened them wide. "I almost forgot my meeting. I need to go."

And she did.

Chapter 12

It was a rush to get to the Sandwich Club. The orientation to travel in China was helpful, and she could have benefitted from a few extra questions. She didn't want to keep Micah waiting or give up any time with him.

He had coffee for them both and a sandwich resembling a Philly cheesesteak but with shaved bulgogi, a spicy Korean steak, to share when she arrived. She was ravenous but forgot her hunger for food as soon as they embraced.

Micah spoke first as they sat together on the same side of the bench. "So, just where overseas is this assignment, and do I really have input as your text implied?"

"It's China. Near Xi'an. I probably will leave right away. Some U.S. engineers and technicians are supposed to be consulting on renewable building materials and architecture. There are some morale problems that prevent much in the way of progress. The whole relationship might have to be scrapped if they can't get some traction."

"Why don't you stay in the states and interview the ones who have left the project?"

"Someone is already on that, and investigation isn't really my role—at least at the inception of a project." Cori was thinking of the times her relentless sense of justice caused her to become the lead investigator on cases. "Does this mean you would prefer that I turn it down?"

"Only if I'm being selfish. It's your decision and always will be. You probably don't know how long it will take."

"No idea. I hope not long."

"You're feeling prepared?"

"This afternoon's session was helpful."

"Are you going with a team?"

"There is one other person I know. He's an accountant. His name is Oryn Greer. This is the first time we'll be working on the same project. The investigator who has been questioning former team members in the states will be joining us at some point as well. I don't know who that is."

"I'm not jealous." He raised his eyebrows and grinned.

"You better be." She giggled.

"How can I get in touch with you?"

"I think in just about any way we do now except the in-person part. Darn it." She scowled. "Our cell phones are supposed to function with any tower."

"We have to learn to navigate these waters, don't we?"

"I guess we do. It's more difficult in practice than in theory."

"Yeah. It's time for my meeting. Be in touch as soon as you know anything."

"I will."

"Are you concerned about Roman?"

She scoffed. "Apparently I am not involved in his health."

"What does that mean?"

"Byron. He came by my office. Roman told him that they need to do this on their own and that I don't need to be involved."

"You're hurt."

"Of course I'm hurt." She was emphatic. She looked away. "People just don't get how I feel."

"I'll say this and risk hurting you more, but you should feel some relief."

"I do feel relief. I was so happy when Roman met the love of his life not only for his happiness, but for the freedom it provided to me. You do realize you are my first relationship in like, maybe forever!" She shook her head slightly back and forth, shut her eyes, and put up her hands as if to defend herself. "You know what, forget it. It's okay. I'll be okay."

"I'm not judging you."

"Don't worry. I'll be fine."

"It never feels good to have people gossip about you."

"Sure. But that's only part of it. I wish they didn't need me, but I have this terrible feeling they really do—or will at some point."

"Do you really think that's the case?"

"I don't know."

"Don't let this fester. You need to talk about it and figure out what's going on."

"I'm afraid of being hurt even more."

"Well said. If you can say that, you can face Roman and Ainsleigh. And Simone for that matter."

"I don't think so."

"I'm so sorry to leave, but I am late. I know you're upset, but are you going to be okay?"

"Yes, go."

"I'll be in touch."

"Sure."

Chapter 13

Cori was ready to confirm with Sophie that she would be accepting the assignment in China when Sophie called to say there would be a delay—perhaps just a couple of days. The investigation stateside was proving to be productive, and the site visit could benefit from its completion. Cori was going to be briefed again in a couple of days. She continued to take on cases that involved emails, telephone contact, and video conferences.

She was in session late in the week when someone interrupted. She called for a break in the session and answered the door to find Blake, her supervisor, standing there.

"Cori, I'm sorry for the interruption. I was told about an emergency call for you from Helen in Arizona. I thought it might be about your brother."

"Oh. I should call, but what about my session?"

"I'll close out the session. Go do what you gotta do."

Cori raced out of her office and called Ainsleigh's cell. There was no answer. She called Roman's cell; still no answer. She didn't know if Helen had a number, and she didn't have the landline for Ainsleigh's parents, so she called the hospital.

"I'm sorry, we can't give out any information."

"Can you tell me if Roman Sellers is a patient there."

"Yes. He was admitted a few hours ago through the Emergency Department."

"If there are any family members there, could you give them a message to call my cell. I am free now and will await a call."

"Yes. I will call his nurse."

Cori wrung her hands and paced the length of her office back and forth and then stopped to stare out of the window. She thought about how cliché her actions were. She wasn't about to tie up her phone by calling anyone else, so she continued to veg; and wait. Besides, what would she say?

A number she didn't recognize lighted up her phone, and she answered it on the first ring. "This is Cori."

"Cori. Hello. This is Helen."

"Hi Helen. I'm sorry it was hard to reach me. What can I do?"

"Roman is having trouble breathing, and everything they have tried doesn't help. Ainsleigh is in the hospital herself with a respiratory infection. That's why I'm calling."

"Do you want me to come?"

"I think you should. Yes."

"I'll get a flight as soon as I can. Is Roman able to sign permission for me to talk to the doctor while I wait?"

"I don't know. We can try."

"Please, try to make it happen. I'll keep the line open for your call. Thank you, Helen. And thank you for being there."

"Bye, Cori."

Cori purchased a ticket online for that evening and started to text Micah. She had to look up in the middle of writing the text to see who had entered her office. It was Claris. "Hello there! How are the bride and groom?"

"We're very good. It all seems like a dream!"

"The wedding was like a dream. And I loved, loved, loved the reception. Very well done!"

"I thought you would love the flow of events."

"You were right."

"How are things, Cori?"

"Not great."

"Uh oh. Tell me about it."

"I have a flight to Arizona tonight. Roman is having trouble breathing, and Helen sounded very alarmed. Ainsleigh is hospitalized as well with an infection, probably brought on by a case of the flu. I need to talk to the doctor, Claris."

"That could be hard if you aren't listed as his proxy or if he hasn't signed a release."

"I'm sure I no longer am on any official documents."

"That's tough. I think you'll be able to find out more when you get there. Does Micah know?"

"I was in the middle of a text to him when a blushing bride strolled into my office!" She proceeded to finish the text.

"How is Micah? Are things still good?"

"Not as good as they were. I don't like being judged."

"What is he judging?"

"My hurt."

"How so?"

"I don't think he understands it, and that I get. But he thinks I need to do something about it. With Roman and Simone."

"Oh." Claris showed her doubt with a scowl.

"Not to put on more pressure, but what about the project we talked about."

"You mean the one we can't talk about?"

"Yes. That one."

"I tried to see myself as a good match. But I just can't. I'm sorry. Claris, are you sure about this yourself?"

"Sure? Of course not! I'm just walking by faith and not by sight."

"You have my admiration and my prayers."

"Definitely we need your prayers; better hold off on the admiration. I don't know how this is going to play out."

"Claris, I need to talk to Blake about my absence. I almost forgot that step. Sorry to rush off, but I'll let you know as soon I have any news."

"Go. Yes. Prayers."

Cori found her supervisor back at her own desk. "Blake, thanks for finishing up the session. How was it?" "It was fine. The client agreed you two had made good progress, and she was good to go for now. So, what's up? Did you reach Helen?"

"Yes. My brother is having trouble breathing, but his wife is too sick to talk and so is he. I'm not an official contact for him. I really would like to fly out tonight."

"I think you need to. I haven't had an update on where the Xi'an project stands. But we'll reassign it if something pops before you are able to return. Go. Take care of your family."

"Thanks. I don't know what else to say."

"You don't have to. Be in touch."

"I will."

She received a text back from Micah as she left Blake's office. "I want to go with you. Which flight are you on?"

Her heart melted. How could she be cold to him? "That's so nice. Let me find out more. Don't put your life on hold just yet! And thanks."

"Okay. Update me with every bit of news. Please."

"Yes."

The ringtone startled her. It was an Arizona area code.

"Dr. Estes here. I'm calling to speak with Roman Seller's sister."

"Yes. This is Cori." *Why do all doctors speak so fast on the telephone?*

"I understand you want an update on your brother, Roman?"

"Yes. Thanks for calling. His wife is sick, and his grandmother is just getting acquainted with his condition."

"I understand. I am the hospitalist and the specialist will be here soon. We're doing all the conventional therapies, but his condition hasn't changed. Tests on his lungs don't show a change from the last time we tested."

"Over the years, he has developed polyps so far into his nasal passage that they're difficult to find, but always manifest in breathing difficulties."

"I'll get back to you."

He hung up. Could Cori assume they hadn't considered it? She cupped her chin in her hands, rubbed her hands over her cheeks and through her hair as if to bring on some breakthrough in understanding. Then she closed the office and made her way home to pack.

She texted Micah when she arrived home. "I spoke with the doctor. I am not enlightened, but I am packed."

"Can I take you to the airport?"

"Did you have plans tonight?"

"I was going to lead a group session."

"Please. Do the session. I've done this many times."

"I'm concerned. I'd rather spend the time with you."

"Too many crises. Too many disruptions. You can always come later."

"Okay for now. Stay in touch."

"You too."

Unlike other times, she made reservations at a long-term parking lot and would board a courtesy shuttle to the airport. She had just arrived at the lot when her cell rang with an Arizona area code once again. She pulled into a parking space and answered.

"Dr. Estes again. He's breathing better. It was a polyp. It was removed. That was good information you provided. Years of experience, I presume."

"I'm so relieved. I'm about to fly out there. Do you think I should?"

"That's up to you and your family. He's very stable. Call him and chat tomorrow."

"Thank you for calling. So much."

I don't know if I need to go. Another paradox? At least it's me saying it to me this time.

By checking back through her calls, she found what she thought was Helen's number and dialed it.

"Hello. Is this Cori?"

"Yes. Helen. I hear things are better."

"Oh, they are dear. The doctor says it's thanks to you. We're so grateful."

"I'm grateful that he's okay. He is, isn't he?"

"Yes. I've seen him. He's on pain meds, but he is breathing well."

"Helen, I have to decide in the next few seconds if I'm coming. What do you think?"

"Ainsleigh's folks are keeping a vigil with her. I am doing my best for Roman, but I am very tired. I don't think I'm much of a help."

"That's what the hospital is for. I think we're too obsessed with hospital vigils. Go home and rest. He's always recovered well from the polyps, unless his compromised health makes it more complicated. Why don't I stay here for now, and you let me know the situation when he is able to come home?"

"Yes. That's makes sense. Thank you dear."

"You bet."

She immediately called the airline and took a voucher. She texted Micah and told him the good news. She went back to the office and found Blake was still there.

"Cori. What are you doing here?"

Cori retorted, "What are you doing here?"

Blake simply rolled her eyes.

Cori answered her question. "It all worked out. I don't need to go right now. Roman is fine for the time being."

"Wow. I was about to consider who I can find for Xi'an. Are you still on board?"

"Yes. Let's do this."

"Okay. You leave from Newark at 8 a.m. the day after next. I think you know that the stateside investigator made good progress and has a bead on what he needs to do for follow-up in Xi'an. They determined that an accountant isn't needed, but we want you to be there to help support the workers. The investigator will meet you at the airport and provide the details on what he's found and how he intends to proceed."

"Who *is* this investigator?"

"I've never met him. It was set up through Legal. Claris may know. I've received my information from Seavers, who has been way too involved if you want to know how I really feel. I'll try to get you the name."

"Thanks."

"Let me know if things change."

"I will. Thanks for being flexible." Cori was thankful for a supervisor like Blake.

Chapter 14

Cori was able to chat with Roman in the morning, who sounded better than he had in a long time.

"Cori, how did you know it was a polyp?"

"History. I'm glad you can forget some of the medical procedures you been through. That said, it would be a lot safer if you had total recall."

"Yeah. There's no way I can ever get through my head all you know about this disease and what it's put you through."

"No comparison, Bro. I'm just a resource and support. You do all the suffering. The only suffering for me is what I feel for you."

"I thought I was preventing that. I guess I made it worse."

"No worries. Just get well."

"I think I am well. I doubt the lung thing is as much of an issue as they thought. It probably was the polyp all along."

"I love your optimism, but I don't think the pictures lie."

"Time will tell."

"You probably haven't seen Ainsleigh."

"I'll be lucky if they let me near her again. The bar is pretty high. Is anyone ever germ-free?"

"No. It must be awful. Do you video-chat?"

"Yes. A lot. She feels better. Probably will go home soon."

"How about you?"

"I would be home by now if I lived alone, with just skilled nursing. It's more complicated with a household of three. Helen may have a place soon. Ainsleigh might have to live with her parents for a while for the sakes of both of us."

"Oh Roman. I know that's awful for you."

"Yeah. I'm willing to bag it and just take a chance. But Ainsleigh would feel so guilty if anything happened, so she won't agree to be reckless."

"I understand the individual viewpoints. I'm glad I have no influence! But I can let you rest. Take care."

She updated Micah the night before about the change in plans, and they decided to have an early dinner. She had plans to leave right after dinner and stay at the Newark airport for her flight the next morning.

She met Micah at a small burger bar. Jessalyn had recommended it and told her it was nothing like the greasy burger joint near the hospital.

They embraced, but there wasn't the excitement for Cori there had been on so many other occasions. She was irked with herself for letting her stubborn attitude interfere with her happiness. *How do I manage to torpedo my chances for happiness? I thought I wanted this so badly.*

"Are you nervous?" Micah spoke first as they sat across from one another.

"I am, but the flurry of activity has kept me from reaching the point of anxiety . . . yet!"

"And Roman? You mentioned it was rather a simple solution?"

"The immediate problem, yes. I'm so thankful. It was just a polyp. It was so far into the sinus cavity that they didn't notice it. It's happened before."

"How *did* they discover it, then?"

"I remembered."

"You told them to look?"

Yes, me! Why do you think I was so hurt to be summarily dismissed from the tribe? And then you judge me because I hurt.

"Cori?"

"Wha- oh, yeah. I guess."

"You saved his life."

"No. It's always the doctors who do that. Everybody else is just peripheral, no matter what."

"You're angry with me."

"It's not important."

"It is to me."

"I'll get over it."

"Is that what you want to do? Set it aside until time has worn it out?"

"Well, what do you want, Micah?"

"I don't want you to be angry."

"I want what you want. So, I'll just stop."

"Cori. Please. "

"I'm not hungry. I'll just get an early start for the airport."

"Please stay. Don't leave like this."

"Don't worry. I'm fine."

He stood up, but he had no intention of detaining her against her will. She was out the door in an instant.

Chapter 15

Cori was incommunicado for the drive to the airport and after check-in at the hotel. She intended to keep her cell off and asked the desk for a wake-up call. She was ashamed for being so upset, but she wasn't prepared to deal with it.

The wake-up call seemed so unreasonable when it chimed. What an awful time to get up. Yet, she was ready quickly having adjusted over time to having her routine change according to her various assignments.

The expense of a hotel room proximate to the airport was worth it, especially since Amity was paying for it—or the client. She arrived at the terminal with ease and turned on her phone when she was checked in and seated near her gate. The cell chimed repeatedly. She had so many texts she didn't know which to read first.

Part of her didn't want to read Micah's. Going dark really was all about him. Yet, she read his first.

"Cori, I'm sorry."

Well why didn't you just say that to begin with, jerk. Delete.

There was one from Jessalyn.

"How was the burger bar? Safe trip!"

There were a few that were just wishing her well. Roman and Ainsleigh both sent her best wishes for a safe travel.

Then she noticed one from Claris.

"Cori. I wanted to let you know that I just found out who is the investigator hired for the Xi'an project. It's . . ."

She hadn't finished the text when she heard a voice say her name that she couldn't quite place.

"Hi Cori. It's good to see you again. I guess we'll be traveling and working together."

She looked up. *Stewart?*

"What are *you* doing here?" She still didn't believe it was Stewart. Stewart, the private investigator who attempted to seduce her for hire by Lourdes Dallas.

"I've been working stateside with the engineers who have abandoned the Xi'an project."

"Amity hired *you?*"

"Yeah. I know you didn't expect they would again. It's a long story."

Under her breath she muttered. "I don't believe this."

"I know you're shocked and probably upset. How can I apologize for what I did? I've tried several times. I've tried to make it up to you."

"Um. Just a minute. I had my cell turned off, so I'm just getting caught up with my texts."

She went back to Claris's text. ". . .Stewart." *Claris knew about this?*

She texted back. "He just appeared. What a shock. You knew about this?"

"I didn't know until this morning that he is going to Xi'an."

"Did you know Amity was hiring him again?"

"That's a long story."

"That's what he said. Claris, I'm really mad!"

"I know. I'm sorry for how this happened. I think you'll understand eventually. I don't know when I'll see you again, but when I do, I'll make sure you understand."

Those long texts always came through as multiple texts, but she got the idea.

She finally stared ahead.

"Are you finished?" Stewart was almost always on the verge of being glib.

"Yes. I'm finished."

"Are you going to be mad at me forever?"

"I think so."

"Oh. Okay. I'm good for it."

It's hard to be mad when folks joke about it. That's one of the antidotes I use in coaching.

"Truce?" He asked tentatively.

"Truce. But you have a long way to go to prove yourself."

"Oh, I'll prove myself over and over. I'm a jerk, I know. The real deal."

She laughed just a little. "So, what can you tell me about this case?"

"These guys have been through the ringer. There are some shenanigans going on, no doubt."

"Do you know what?"

"No. They don't either. We might not get to the bottom of it, exactly. But no matter what designs the teams put together for site specifications, the feasibility reports come back with problems. They have architectural plans under way, and they're working hard on developing a green building. But progress on the site and energy provisions keep getting stalled. We need to suss out every bit of detail we can. Nothing will be accomplished if experienced people keep leaving."

"I know nothing about architecture, energy, green materials, construction, or any of that."

"They do. We have to get them willing to work as a team within their group and with the local engineers, and I think they'll be able to get on with the project."

"I usually go into a project more confident than I feel right now."

"Well right now, we'd better go through the gate. They're calling our flight!"

Chapter 16

66 Okay if I sit with you?" Stewart never hesitated to appear submissive.

"We can start out that way. The situation will be reassessed at regular intervals."

He laughed. "Then I'm in trouble before I start. Have you ever been on a flight this long?"

"Not quite."

"Same."

"Small talk?"

Cori smiled. "How about telling me what else you know about Xi'an?"

"We're staying in Xi'an at one of the larger chains . . ."

"The Hilton."

"Yeah. The Hilton. Anyway, the actual work site is in a smaller town in the Shaanxi Province. It's a huge construction company that's retooling for renewable construction. A new generating plant is planned for the immediate area, and they want to use it as a prototype for the boom they're expecting in the energy business. According to most reports, China's coal-powered plants are cleaner than most in the world, but this area is functioning with a bunch of old, small plants that are inefficient, dirty and can't seem to prevent the brownouts that happen all too frequently."

"Are there specific complaints from the former team members?"

"Mostly what I've told you. The team leader has been there from the get-go and wants to stay the course. To a person, the staff said they sense he's trying but totally ineffective. If we can't help, the company that provided the temporary workers and Amity will pull out. They'll forfeit a lot of the contracted money, so it's not what they want."

"What's your approach?"

"I want someone to explain the times and events that cause the snags."

"So, are you going to look at plans first?"

"Everything. Documents, talk to people, site visits. I think we should get everyone together for breakfast. I emailed the idea and asked for them to meet at the hotel. I told the hotel, too. We have a conference room and a buffet."

"I think that's a good idea. I'm ashamed to admit I'm relieved that we're starting out on the closest thing to our own turf." Cori wanted to feel confident. She didn't.

"Exactly. I've never traveled in China before."

"Nor have I."

"Are you worried?"

"I'm trying not to think about the apprehensions I grew up with."

"Yeah. I think beyond the issue we're going there to address, we better keep any opinions to ourselves."

"What *are* your opinions?"

"Are you baiting me?"

"No." She smiled. "It doesn't help that I just read the book, *Shanghai Faithful*, by the great-niece of Watchman Nee. He was both a preacher and an inspirational writer before and after the Party took control of China in 1947. He was imprisoned on charges that would be laughable if the situation wasn't so horrible. He was in prison for 20 years until his death.

"Added to that was the way his extended family was treated. His niece had her career as a concert pianist destroyed. They tried to wear down the family by taking away their possessions—starting with the piano. They continued in waves until they took away anything that mattered including any reading materials. Most of their furniture was destroyed or taken away, even beds from the elderly. His sister was systemically beaten to get her to confess to bogus crimes. She never did.

"I know it was a half a century ago, but 50-year-old crimes are being discussed and 'tried' in the U.S. media whenever it impacts policy in the direction they're purveying at the time." Cori used a scoffing tone.

"Hey, you're talking to a libertarian, here. I need no convincing. I'm the only one left in my generation who understands at some level the effort to stop communism from spreading. People who knew what Watchman Nee was going through at the time, exponentially multiplied by the number of countries in the throes of communist influence or domination, couldn't help but support the effort to fight its conquest of human freedoms and rights. I know if I had lived at the time, I would have been sympathetic. I get the criticism about involvement in foreign conflicts and backing questionable regimes. It's just too bad that most folks will mindlessly accept views according to the dictums of a drunken character on a tv show without ever letting themselves feel the gut-wrenching facts about the human suffering at the hands of some real madmen." He took a breather, and then changed his tone. "Enough politics. But watch out. I hear the Second World may be making a comeback."

"Thank you. But I understand your point. My parents were politically conservative and talked about the turmoil and controversies of their youth. And, here we are, headed for China. I don't know what my parents would say if they were alive. Come to think of it, not too much shocked them. They would have taken it in stride, pretty much."

She was abrupt in changing the subject. "By the way, are you still working for Lourdes Dallas?"

"No. I told her about Reina, as you asked. Then I told her I wouldn't be available."

"Huh."

"Have there been any other problems?"

"No, but it doesn't mean it's over. Just a lack of opportunity."

"Why wouldn't it be over?"

Darn. How do I explain? I never told him about my adoption.

"Oh, I wasn't sure if she would accept the explanation."

"It's never made sense how harassing you would make anything better for her." He detested situations where he couldn't solve the problem.

"Isn't it what she does . . . delights in throwing shade on others?"

"Is there any way to stop her?"

"I can't and shouldn't diagnose without more information. But, in my opinion, she could benefit from DBT—dialectical behavior training or therapy."

"I think she's diabolical enough without any training."

Cori smiled. "Dialectical. It's one of the most often recommended training for borderline personality disorder."

"Oh, she has a disorder alright. Nothing borderline about it."

Cori was quite entertained by his humor. "Borderline is the disorder."

Stewart changed the subject as if something had just occurred to him. "How is your brother, by the way?"

"He's been through a rough time. He's improved, but it's very probable he's headed for a lung transplant."

"Ugh! You seem matter-of-fact about it. I thought you were super-involved."

"Less than I used to be. I still care, a lot."

"Yeah. Of course. Anything or anyone new in your life?" Stewart didn't hold back on opinions or questions.

"I thought so. It's a little harder than I thought it would be."

"It usually is. What's he do?"

Cori explained Micah's new role and how they met.

"What's the problem?"

"I am."

"Your fiery personality, no doubt. No one gets you."

"Well. Something like that." He was too accurate, and she didn't like it.

"I do."

"You don't even know me."

"I know enough."

"You miss a lot." Cori was emphatic.

"I *have* missed things, but not much. You create a whirlwind when the situation is sketchy. That creates a lot of fallout. People can't take it. You need someone who understands you."

"Like you do." Her tone was mocking.

"See?"

"Are you hitting on me again?"

"Yup. This time for real and for free."

She wanted to slap him. She considered it for a moment but laughed instead and shook her head in disbelief. After a short pause, she said, "I have some reading to do. Maybe this is a good time to take a break."

"Oh, I have the names of the clients and short bios. Here they are. There are summaries of the other folks I interviewed, too."

"That's good. I'm never this unprepared. This will help."

The first leg of their journey was 15 hours. They had time to stretch in Beijing before the last two hours to Xi'an. They arrived mid-evening on the day after their take-off from Newark. They checked in and said good night.

Chapter 17

It had been a long time since their last meal, so Cori ordered poached eggs and toast from room service, plugged in her cell phone, and then fell into bed. She hadn't showered or unpacked, she only washed up and put on her pajamas while awaiting the eggs.

Her cell alarm woke her up out of a sound sleep, but she didn't feel rested. She felt disorient and dread. She craved adventure seventy-five percent of the time and feared it the rest.

She emerged from the shower to a text.

"This is Stewart. Breakfast at 8:00 a.m.." She added him to her contacts with the "When Will I Be Loved" song as the ringtone. It was the first few words of the song that were pertinent, and it also was the Karaoke song they had performed together.

She texted back "Okay. What room? Do I need to bring anything?" "The Terra Cotta room down the hall to the left of the elevators on this floor. The hotel supplies everything."

"Got it!"

She understood the local climate was not much warmer than home. She brought several pants suits, and she had a shawl in the event the meeting room was cooler than what she was accustomed to indoors.

Cori arrived early and chose a seat facing the doors in the middle of the massive table. The rest of the room was as ornate as the table. There was a marble fireplace festooned in gold trim. The coffered ceiling was painted white with green insets; there was green striped wall paper extending down to meet raised paneling on the bottom half of the wall. It wasn't tired, but fresh and new looking, even if it seemed from a different era and wasn't to her taste. She was still taking in her surroundings when the food arrived. She stood up to greet the servers and found that one of them spoke English. As they chatted, Stewart arrived followed by a steady stream of folks until all had arrived. Besides Stewart and her, there were five men and two women.

Stewart took charge, introduced himself and Cori and asked the others to choose a chair and start introductions. They went around the table, and folks were asked to wear name tags just for the first meal together. Still not having taken a seat, Stewart invited everyone to help themselves to eggs, pancakes, toast, and scones. There were hot beverages and water.

Cori didn't return to her seat after picking up a scone. Instead, she walked around and chatted with people until everyone was sated. Stewart was aware when most people had bussed their plates and were holding only coffee cups, so he brought the meeting to order.

He explained the work he had done in the states and asked that everyone give him a thorough account of their observations and concerns. He requested help from anyone who could review the volumes of paperwork.

Cori explained her role to provide support as they tried to embark on a road to solutions and encouraged them to acknowledge if there was any fallout from what had gone on before. There was a private room set aside for sessions requiring confidential exchanges.

Her statement reminded Stewart that he also wanted to offer private interviews with everyone in due time, and he let people know.

The noise level wasn't deafening, but it was loud. For hours they managed to listen, take notes, clarify, and compare accounts to keep tabs on the most repeated complaints. Cori had read through dozens of document pages when one of the women asked to talk alone, so they excused themselves.

Cori showed Ava North to a seat and gave her a moment. Ava said nothing, and Cori broke the silence. "I've forgotten your role on the team, Ava."

"I'm one of the engineers who creates the schematics. I'm supposed to be working on the efficiency of the energy delivery systems. I think there is this one plant that is the roadblock to whatever progress I try to make. We just can't get accurate data from them on their service areas, billing, receipts, or anything. Nothing about the data adds up. We've tried piecing it together with what is not covered by the other plants, but that's ridiculous."

"Do you think people are worried about losing their jobs with the closing of inefficient plants?"

"They've been told they can transfer when the time comes."

"So, is your concern with this plant what brings you to this session? You think all of this is a waste of time until they cooperate?"

"Yes. But that's not the only thing I wanted to add."

There was a long pause. Cori was familiar with the pause. It meant Ava was unsure whether it was a good idea to proceed. Sometimes clients feared a personal toll and sometimes they wondered why bother when nothing would come of it.

"Ava. Is this confidential?"

"There would be no purpose in telling you unless you are willing to follow up."

"I'm just the person. I'm always willing to take relevant action that's within my power."

Ava chuckled. "Coming here was the most daring thing I've ever done. I'm not an adventurer. I've almost quit so many times."

"Something is keeping you here."

"I'm not a quitter. I want to do a good job, if that's possible, and that has been in doubt many times. I also want to see if more time would allow me to sense whether there is any significance to what I've observed going on with some of the employees from that particular plant."

"And that is . . ."

Ava took a deep breath and closed her eyes. She threw her head back and looked up and to the side as if she had dreaded Cori's question. "There's a lot of talk about the number of people who have left our team. But that's nothing compared to turnover of the staff from that place."

"Tell me about it. I haven't heard anyone mention this or that you had much interaction with local employees."

"At my level, we don't. Neil Reynolds does the liaison work with local employees. But . . . I know this sounds stupid . . . I go through the main factory of that plant to get to the rest-room. I'm afraid I'm a frequent flyer. I'm good with faces and names. There is a huge turnover . . . mostly the women. They all are so young. I've heard a rumor they are recruited from the poorer, rural areas. I'm just afraid they are being harassed or something."

"That's troubling."

"Yeah! Productivity has to be impacted by the turnover."

"Have you said anything to Neil?"

"Not for a long time. He has so many problems without add-ing this to his plate. I mentioned it rather off-hand. I think he's too overwhelmed. He didn't really respond to me."

"We're going to check this out, Ava. Thanks. Is there any-thing else? Did you get to know any of the local employees?"

"No. In fact, counterparts don't interact with me at all. I take the calculations as best I can and submit my drawings. I think they consider most of them. There are interpreters and local employees who speak English, but they never ask questions or seek me out for any reason. If they had a choice, I don't think they would use my schematics. I've never sensed that they are concerned about precision, efficiency, or any of the goals we thought were part of our mission."

"Thanks. I'm glad we spoke. Let me know if there is anything else that comes to light or that you might not have mentioned."

On their way back to the group they chatted about whether anyone on the team had been able to see some of the sights while in the Province. "Some of us took part of a day to explore the Terra Cotta Soldiers. Seeing the Great Wall has been on my bucket list since I can remember, but I'll have to work it in to my return trip. The strong recommendation is to see it from Beijing, which is almost seven hundred miles. So, it makes sense to split the trip home in two. Fly to Beijing, do some exploring, and then fly home from there."

Cori couldn't help making a crack. "An obvious field trip for a group of engineers!"

They both laughed.

Cori and Stewart's eyes met as Cori and Ava rejoined the group. They held the gaze for a moment, and finally Stewart said. "We need to talk." Cori agreed.

Stewart provided projects for small groups scouring some of the documents while he and Cori chatted.

Stewart provided her the chance to talk first. "Did Ava shed any light on what's going on?"

"Let's go to the interview room." Cori started walking before he issued a response.

Cori recapped the important points as she saw them. "Young female employees come and go quickly in this one plant. It's Ava's opinion that the plant is preventing the team from getting a handle on what areas are serviced by the plant and can't complete their work until they have accurate information."

Stewart froze. Then he sucked in a breath through his teeth. "This isn't good."

"What do you think is up? Did you turn up something?"

"The billing data for that plant is way off from the energy produced, which is way off from the energy consumed. Government officials knew something was off, but this plant is small potatoes in the scheme of things. They thought some consultation time could take care of any problems. The owners balked, but they're involved in so many plants they just let it all happen. They blamed it on design capabilities that prevent efficiency in delivery and lost power. It doesn't take a forensic accountant to know there is graft, and I can't believe no one discovered it before now. That was one of the biggest issues I found until something I just heard coupled with what you just told me."

"What did you hear?"

"One of the engineers was working late one night. He saw a van leave one of the warehouses previously reported as abandoned. He didn't see what was loaded in it. It had been backed up to the side door. All he saw were the double doors of the panel van close and it took off.

"I looked at supply manifests and inventory reports for the last few weeks, and nothing indicated that the building was used for storage. I'm headed over there with Neil. I think I'll advise him to keep everyone else in the hotel until further notice."

"This is human trafficking, isn't it?"

Stewart dropped his hands to the table and hung his head for a second before looking up at her. It wasn't a theatrical move; more one of dread. "I thought you might see it."

"I'm going to help."

"No. There is nothing for you to do."

"Why? What are you going to do?"

"I don't know. But I can't let this go."

"Let's get started and see where it takes us."

"This isn't the U.S., Cori. We have very little in the way of protection. Hell, we don't even know our way around here. We have no law enforcement backing us up."

"You stay, I stay. I'm going to call the U.S. Embassy in Beijing. You do whatever was your next step. I'll use my room for privacy, and I'll notify Legal at Amity. I hope I can get through to Claris."

"Good idea. The consulates in Chengdu and Jianghan are closer, and we may want the U.S. team to go to one of them until things settle down, if they do, but I want the Embassy contacted and they can decide who responds."

"Got it."

Cori had the number as part of the emergency package Amity prepared before she left. She explained the situation to the best of her ability, and she was met with dead silence each time she was transferred to a new desk. It seemed forever when she was connected to an assistant in the office of the deputy ambassador. She didn't know much about embassy operations, but that seemed pretty far up the food chain.

"This is Scott Perry."

Cori lunged into the situation and didn't take a breath until she leveled all the relevant issues on him. She even asked his advice.

"I agree that it's best to halt work for now. I will call the local authorities and have them begin an investigation. A call from my office will bring some accountability from the inception of the investigation. I'll also notify our minister of FEP, that is the Fossil Energy Protocol, in case they have connections in the region. Offhand, I'm not familiar with the plant, of course, nor of its ownership. I think it's safe to get a flight to Beijing and then the U.S. from there if you and any of the others want to leave. Let me know when the flight or flights are obtained. I'm going to tell our security team to issue an alert. Give me all of the names, telephone numbers, and U.S. agencies involved that you know of."

She gave him everything she knew and said she would call back with more information.

She rushed back to the meeting room and found it in controlled chaos. Neil was making travel arrangements, and several were putting the documents back in order. One man was on a telephone call and finally with the cell in one hand and the other hand blocking his ear, took his call into the hallway. Cori sensed he was talking to the firm that had sent them. Soon after she walked into the room, several exited to cancel their hotel rooms and pack.

There were two people she didn't see. No Stewart and no Ava. She scoured the room when her eyes spied Stewart emerging from the interview room. He caught her eye immediately and headed in her direction.

He simply raised his brows and tilted his head near her. She knew he wanted to know what went on with the Embassy call. She provided a quick summary. "You didn't tell him some of us are staying?"

"No. We talked about leaving as an option, but I'm surprised everyone is bolting. I'll make sure they know some of us are staying. We might need their help."

Then she added, "What are we doing next?"

"You have an airline reservation along with the rest of them."

"Well, it's a waste. I'm not going yet."

"Cori."

"I was meant to do this. I was just too cowardly to see it."

"Meaning?"

"I had a chance to work on a task force."

"Claris and Trent?"

Cori addressed him in an emphatic whisper, "What?" She looked around, and quieted. "You know about that?"

He shrugged. "Yeah. I shouldn't be talking about it. I roped them in. So, they asked you."

It was more of a statement than a question.

Cori was incredulous but tried to stay in control. "What are you talking about?"

"It was my idea," he confessed.

Cori closed her eyes as if in disgust, or simply as if she was baffled. "Explain."

"Come back to the interview room." As he proceeded, he glanced around the room to be sure the chaos was still controlled.

"I've been an extractor of trafficked humans for years."

"I didn't know . . ."

"No one should know."

"Lourdes? The Cape?"

"All true. Lourdes alone nearly financed the job; she just didn't know it. That's why I accepted all of those absurd assignments."

"I thought extractors charged mega-bucks."

"A lot of them, yes. But their clients are the rich ones whose kids have been duped into running away. They're willing and able to pay big bucks to get them back. Which is fine. It's important work. There are tons of cases that don't fit that profile."

"Now I really don't understand why you would agree to try to seduce me. Isn't that what you're trying to combat, even if on a low level?"

"I never intended to seduce you. Now that you know me better, I hope you'll believe me. I didn't try to explain it before, but now you know my real convictions."

"How far did you determine you would take it?"

"I didn't plan to go through the hotel door. But I knew you wouldn't anyway."

"How could you know that?"

"It's what I do."

"If you know so much about people, why would you deal with someone like Lourdes."

"To finance my work. I've known all along she has issues."

Cori shook her head. "Anyhow, what now?"

"I'm going out to the site. I'll let the local police know, but I'm not waiting for them. Would you go make sure everyone's flights are in order and that they have plans to get to the airport?"

"Wait for me."

"No, Cori."

"I'll just follow you right now without checking on the others."

"Okay. I'm going to ask at the desk for an interpreter. I'll be right back."

Cori went back to the conference room. She wanted to ask Neil if all of the documents had pulled together. She spied him gathering the documents. "How are the flight plans coming?"

Neil looked up. "They're all set. The hotel van is going to take everyone to Xianyang. The flight isn't for a couple of hours, but I think it's the best place for everyone. I think you know I'm staying. Everyone has checked out of the hotel except Stewart and me, and I'll hold onto these documents."

Cori added. "Do you have the most significant ones earmarked? I think I should fax them to the Embassy."

"You need to get going."

"I'm not going. Here's the deal, you fax the docs while I let them know I still need my room."

"Does Stewart know?"

"He will." She looked around. "Neil. Have you seen Ava?"

"Actually, no. Not for a long time. Could you ask around while I do this?"

"Sure." Cori asked the others, and no one had seen her for a long time. She went to the main desk and saw Neil at the business center. She remembered she hadn't given him the Embassy fax, so she went over and wrote it on a face sheet for him. "No one has seen Ava for a long time, Neil. They don't have a clue where she is. I'm about to ask at the desk."

"Thanks. I'll be there as soon as this is done."

Cori approached the registration desk and asked if anyone spoke English. An enthusiastic young woman greeted Cori and asked what she could do for her.

"I need to know if anyone has spoken to Ava North or left any messages or anything about her location?"

"Okay." The energetic woman asked everyone separately and soon returned to Cori.

"Ava went to work. She had to get something there."

"Thank you."

Cori dialed Stewart, who immediately picked up. "What is it Cori?"

"Ava went to the plant. We have to leave now. Where are you by the way?"

He swore. "Yeah. We do. I just finished with the police." Then he appeared around the corner. No longer on the cell, he rushed a question, "Where's Neil?"

"Faxing docs to the Embassy. Here he is now. Neil, did you get them done? I'll get them into the hotel safe. We have no more time to spare; Ava is at the worksite. I've been trying to reach her since I first noticed she's missing, but no answer."

Neil piped up. "We have a rental car. It's a sh**-bucket, but it gets us around. Let's go."

Stewart was on his way and while in motion said, "I have two small tracking devices. Neil, take one; Cori, here's the other. Just in case."

Neil acted surprised. "You came prepared!"

Neither Cori nor Stewart said anything in response to his comment. Cori had one more request.

"Go check on the others and tell them not to wait for me or Ava. I'm going to visit the ladies' room one more time."

Stewart looked peeved but said nothing as he and Neil headed to the conference room.

She was back in the lobby before they were.

Stewart stayed in motion and showed his impatience. "This is it. They're fine. We're going."

This was Cori's first glimpse of the Middle Kingdom during the day. The city of Xi'an was bustling at this hour, and it took some time to drive out of the city. She had never seen a place like it. There were large districts with buildings that were several stories high and showcased the traditional rooflines characteristic of Asian countries for decades. Skyscrapers rose beyond the blocks of hipped Chinese and double eave roofs. The contrast was stark. The Hilton was on a street that, all told, was ten lanes. There were islands separating nearly every couple of lanes, and Cori was relieved to have a driver. They had a glimpse of the ancient city wall and the Big Goose Pagoda. Eventually the cityscape gave way to a rural area, and she could see a mountain in the distance. They traveled toward the mountain, but never came near before stopping at the coal-fired plant. It was larger than Cori had anticipated.

Neil drove to the administrative offices, parked, and headed inside. Stewart was close behind and Cori in their wake. Someone who seemed in charge came out to meet Neil and shook his hand. The man Cori speculated was Zhang Bao, Neil's counterpart. Though she couldn't hear what they were saying, she could tell they communicated without speaking the language of the other. The interpreter helped when they became stuck. After some discussion, Bao shook his head and led them all outside.

Cori followed like a puppy having no idea what was discussed. After a considerable walk outside the plant, they came to an abandoned-looking building. Bao unlocked the door, and they all walked in. As if on cue, each took out their cells to use as flashlights. If there were any windows, they were covered up or painted over. Cori was thankful for the faint light. If fully illumined, she would have thrown up. The filth and stench were atrocious, and it was obvious that human beings had occupied the space as living quarters in the very recent past.

Bao was stupefied, or he was the best actor in the Shaanxi province. Stewart instructed Bao to find better flashlights or floodlights and bring them back to the storage area. He suggested that Neil and Cori step out for fresh air. They all did.

Darkness was beginning to settle outside as well. No one spoke. Stewart embraced Cori, who was shaken by what she saw. Bao returned, and they all took a light and went back inside. Cori wasn't sure how long she would last in the storage area—physically or emotionally. There was evidence of human excrement of all kinds, including rags for women who had their menses while there. There was one old sink, no stove, and no evidence of conventional dining utensils. There were some small pails, and Cori wouldn't let herself think of all the uses those vessels had served.

She was only glancing around the room while the others were overturning blankets, old ordinance used for the plant, pails, rags, and other detritus when she spied something near the entrance. It was several sheets of paper folded in fourths. She scrambled over to pick it up and stepped outside to read what she had found.

She cried Stewart's name. He came running outside and saw that she was reading a document he knew she hadn't been holding before. "What is it?"

"This is what Ava came back for."

"Can you tell what it is?"

"It only has some equations and calculations that mean nothing to me. How about you, Neil?" By then Neil had rushed outside as well. She handed him the document.

"It doesn't seem like anything special to me, but it also does look like some of Ava's work. Why would she come back for this?"

Cori had an urgency to her words. "Worse than that, where is she? It looks too much like she was in that godawful room, and they've taken her wherever they take women."

Bao gasped. "What women? What are you saying?"

Stewart spelled it out for him, and Bao looked as though he would faint. He bent over and held his knees. He emerged from that position as if enraged. "Have you called the police you 'ben dan' people?" This more than implied he thought they were stupid. Cori had no idea how he summoned up the sentence in English.

"Yeah we did!" There was a bit of a mocking tone to his response. "More than an hour ago. You see how seriously they are taking the situation. Maybe you should call now that there is more evidence. The U.S. Embassy has been notified as well." The interpreter repeated the information for Bao.

Bao rushed off to his office, and Stewart turned toward the others. "Neil, you and the interpreter stay with Bao and tell the police that these grifters were cooking the books to finance this slavery enterprise going on right under their noses."

Neil took off after Bao, and Stewart turned to Cori.

"I found some notes that obviously weren't part of the official files. They were handwritten in Russian. I suspect these degenerates have access to a small airport that doesn't ask questions. Along with the data, I found some notes that seemed random and unrelated. They were map coordinates. I had time to check and it was in Kazakhstan. Almaty. Surprising. They are doing better than most according to the state department's TIP report. Uzbekistan or Turkmenistan I would expect as a guess."

"TIP?" Cori asked.

"Trafficking in Persons." Stewart quickly responded.

"Any ideas?" Cori was lost. She was glad that Stewart had a clue, but only a very small clue.

"It won't be an airport with international flights."

"Would the Embassy notify possible airports there and where they might be flying from in China?"

"Try your friend. See if he can make it happen. There probably is just enough time."

Cori spoke as she stepped away to make the call. "On it."

Stewart called Legal at Amity. "Claris please."

"Speaking. Stewart? Wh-?"

"There's trouble, Claris. We think a trafficking ring has local workers *and* Ava North, one of the American consultants. Not everyone in the plant is involved, but it's being kept open just for this purpose, funded by graft. We think they'll fly out of a small airport in the south province with the end game being sales in Kazakhstan, starting in Almaty. The evidence is sketchy, but there is some. Cori is trying to get an assistant in the deputy's office at the Embassy in Beijing to alert the airports without international flights. Coordinate with my service on a couple of GPS serial numbers to follow, too. Do something if you can, okay?" He gave her the serial numbers.

"I will. Stay safe."

He was just disconnecting when bullets started flying. He leaped toward Cori, who had moved out of hearing distance to make her call. He grabbed her and sheltered her around the corner of the building. His heart racing, he scoured the landscape to determine where the shooting originated, but he couldn't tell. Then he felt it. Cold iron against his temple, and he hadn't seen it coming. Another armed man came around the corner and grabbed Cori around the mouth. The first man used his barrel to knock Stewart to the ground, and they started searching through his clothing and beyond. They took everything; cell, wallet, belt, pocket knife, everything. Dragging his unconscious body and yanking Cori along with them, they shoved them into a white van, tied them up, and sped off the premises.

Cori was petrified. She wished she had been knocked unconscious too so that she wouldn't have to experience this. The one who wasn't driving came back and searched her too. He searched her thoroughly, and she couldn't help but wonder if she would be violated in other ways as well. When he found nothing except what he had found on Stewart, he took the belongings and kicked her hard in the side. Then he went back to his seat in the front of the vehicle.

Cori wasn't blindfolded for any of this and could see some of what was happening. But it didn't help to know where they were nor where they were headed. It was clear they had traveled over and down a mountain range to get to the plane.

The airport was remote, and the plane they boarded was in the middle of a field. It didn't appear that the original captors had boarded after they loaded her and Stewart as though they were cargo. She couldn't help but wonder what they would do with Stewart. She was quite sure what was her fate, but she couldn't let herself think it would really come to that.

She was cold, her side ached where she had been kicked, and she was frantic; but she couldn't think of anything she could do. She wanted to check on Stewart, but it was difficult to move. It was so dark. She inched toward him, or she thought it was him, calling his name.

Soon after take-off, Stewart surfaced. Entertainment media always made a head gash look benign, but this one was anything but benign. She could tell even in the dark. It took him a few moments to speak.

"We're on a plane, right?"

"Yes."

"Did they hurt you?"

"Not in any way that matters, yet. Let's not talk in case they can hear us."

"Okay."

He fell back asleep, and Cori wondered if he would wake up again. Cori wasn't prayed up. She prayed. She whispered the words because, like the Lord's disciples, she had trouble staying focused in silent prayer. She prayed a long time.

An abrupt bump brought her out of her prayer, and it hurt her sore side. *I fell asleep. I don't know where prayer ended and sleep took over.* She looked around, and she saw Stewart sitting up close to her.

She whispered, "How long have you been awake?"

"Not long at all. I think we're landing." He mouthed words that she couldn't make out at first. Finally, she knew he was saying a protracted "T-R-A-C-K-E-R?"

She more mouthed than whispered, "Intact."

He scowled as if to question how that happened, when the door flew open, and he was dragged out and tossed aside. With his hands behind his back, he found it difficult to stay upright. He fell to the ground and struggled to get up again. Cori was heaved next to him. As if on cue, Stewart and Cori both started crawling away in doomed effort to get away. In a stunning turn of events, men in uniforms appeared out of nowhere, descended on the captors, and quickly cuffed them.

Cori wanted to feel relief, but she had no idea where they were or whether these men were liberators or represented a new level of captivity. Captors 1.0 were being taken away as the wrist bindings were being cut from Stewart and Cori by possible captors 2.0. Stewart bellowed, and everyone acted startled. "Does anyone speak English?"

The man who had cut Stewart free said. "Yes." It was English. *Fingers crossed that isn't the extent of his English.*

"How did you know where we were?"

"GPS."

Spare the details!

Stewart tried again. "These men brought abducted women into the country earlier today."

"We are looking for them. We will take you to a hotel until your flight home."

"Thank you."

They were put in the back of a funny-looking car. Cori thought it looked like a cardboard cutout. They traveled quickly to a hotel, were escorted to the registration desk, and then to their room. One room.

"At least there are two beds." Stewart smirked and headed for the bathroom to clean his wound.

Cori couldn't think of anything to say. She forced a nervous laugh. When Stewart returned with a face cloth and towel she said, "I don't know why I'm laughing. We have no idea whether we're still captives or not. But I'm going to use the bathroom if you don't mind."

"Take your time."

She felt a bit fresher having taken a sponge bath. She didn't know why, but she couldn't imagine a shower and putting back on her filthy clothes. So, she just washed up, rescued the transmitter from its hiding place, and dressed again. She took it out of the tampon and threw the tampon away. She emerged with the transmitter couched in a clean face cloth, and immediately gasped at the sight of food.

"Did you order room service?"

"No. It simply arrived."

"Americans are so used to choices. Kazaks probably think choice is highly overrated!"

"Come on. Let's see what it is. What do you have in the face cloth?"

"The transmitter. I don't think you want to touch it given where it was."

"Where is that?"

"Tampon."

Stewart laughed. "Clever. Very well done. That's why you disappeared to use the bathroom."

"Yeah. Now I'm glad I did for two reasons! Little did I know how long it would be before I used one again!"

He moved toward her and embraced her gently, knowing her side hurt. "Thanks. You saved our lives and maybe the lives of some of the others."

She stayed in his embrace long enough to know it felt good. But she already knew that from the first time. Making no effort to move from him, she quipped, "Ah, we *think* we're saved. We don't really know that! They took our cellphones. I hope we can use the hotel phone?"

"Let's eat, and then let's try."

"Yes!"

Poached eggs and toast. Cori loved poached eggs and toast, which is a good thing. They devoured everything as if it was a race.

"Where should we call first?" Cori wanted to call Claris, but she wanted Stewart's input. They had permission to use the hotel phone.

"It's mid to late afternoon at Amity, and it's early morning in Xi'an. It's a little later in Beijing at the Embassy. I vote for Claris first." He moved to the telephone. He was surprised how quickly he was hearing Claris's voice.

"Claris. It's Stewart. We're okay, but we don't know if we're still captives or not." He said it in earshot of the hotel staff.

"What a relief to hear from you. And you are no longer captives. Someone from the Embassy in Beijing will be there in the morning to escort you to the airport and travel with you for a medical exam. I think Cori spoke with him."

"Why Beijing and not Almaty?"

"Probably both. But it has to do with the women who were abducted!"

"Okay."

"Nice work, you two."

"It was all Cori. I can't wait for her to tell you about it. I won't be repeating the story myself. Seriously, though. I really hate to leave without Ava. I'm worried sick about her."

"Good news. They located her. Corruption can be anywhere. But part of corruption among authorities is a desire to look like heroes. No doubt key authority figures were looking the other way while this was going on but were happy to emerge as conquerors when international attention was at stake. She'll be at your hotel soon and will return to the states with you. Several young women were found at the same time as Ava and were rescued too. You all will be guests of the Embassy."

"What about Neil and Bao?" Cori interrupted, and Stewart relayed the question.

"They were fine. They heard the gunfire and knew right away you were missing. They got the license plate number and headed to the police station."

"The police whom I called at least an hour before?" Stewart sounded miffed, and he was.

"Yeah. They made a flurry of calls including the Embassy and Neil's company. Neil's company called Amity. This all happened within 20 minutes of your disappearance. You would have had someone chasing your trail, but without the GPS tracker, we may always have been several steps behind. Good for Cori."

"Thanks Claris. We can't wait to hear the whole story."

"It's still unfolding. We don't know how long this ring has been in existence, but the records you confiscated might tell us more. We'll get to all that. Good night for now. To Cori too. Oh, the desk should have a cell for you."

"Good to know. They could have told us. Thanks. Night."

Someone from the desk gave them a cell and went back with them to the room.

Chapter 18

"I still can't believe we're okay." Cori confessed. "I feel as though I'm being thankless or something."

"I think that's reasonable until we're home. Even then, the world will be different for you. That's why we wanted you to work with us. We need your skills."

There was a knock on the door. Stewart held his index finger to his lips and moved toward the door. He peered out the peep hole and quickly unlatched the door.

Ava slowly entered the door and fell into Stewart's embrace. Cori joined them, gently touching Ava's shoulder. Ava said nothing but cried silently. Then there were audible sobs. Cori led her to be seated on the bed to keep her from fainting.

Eventually she quieted a bit. Stewart was the first to speak. "How did they hurt you?"

Ava blew her nose, and her voice still sounded tear-laden when she spoke. "Mostly by scaring me to death. So much time was spent moving and traveling that there wasn't time for outright violation or abuse. We were treated roughly, in fact that's an understatement. But when I think of what was ahead." She cried softly again. Ava recovered and looked around. "I don't mean to sound ungrateful, but are we sure we're safe here?"

Cori smiled. "We've been wondering the same thing, but we think so. We spoke with the legal department where I work in the states, and a close colleague was confident that a U.S. Consulate staff member was on his way to escort us home. We're hoping enough people are aware of the situation so that they won't try anything illicit. Ava, can you tell us what happened?"

"I feel like I asked for this by going back there. I used the documents as an excuse; they really weren't that important. But I wanted to check out that storage area. I was trying to get in when I heard shouts inside. I yelled back that I would go for help. When I turned around, that's when I was grabbed."

"How did you get there?" Stewart inquired.

"I took a taxi."

"What happened to that taxi?" He inquired again.

"I don't know. I asked the driver to wait. I've been thinking maybe he had something to do with why I've been rescued."

"The yellow-bellied coward." Stewart's eyes popped out as he realized what he said could be interpreted as a racial slur. It was inadvertent.

"How *did* you find me?" For the first time, Ava asked a question.

Cori gently explained what had transpired from their viewpoint. She didn't edit the details about how the tracker was hidden, and Stewart winced a little. He was quite bold about most things but was a little quirky about certain limits he would push.

Ava was gracious. "Thank you so much for coming after me."

Cori was quick to provide reassurances about the situation. "Ava, you have helped so many with your bravery. I'm sorry for what you have suffered."

"But I put you in danger."

"We would have explored the storage shed based on what someone else told us. We put ourselves in danger. That's not on you. You didn't tell me about the storage area."

"I wanted to find out if I was inflating the story before saying more."

Stewart changed the subject. "I want you both to take the beds. There are two extra blankets in the wardrobe. I'll take the floor."

Both Ava and Cori agreed they could share a bed. Stewart railed against their suggestion. "No way. After what you two have been through, you're not compromising any more privacy!"

Ava nervously vocalized another worry. "Where are the women who were with me?"

Stewart thought for a second and then sighed, "I guess I need to make another call."

He called the registration desk first, and they reassured him that they were in another room in the hotel. He called Claris to see if she had the same information.

Claris confirmed that's what she had been told as well by the U.S. Embassy in Almaty, which was now involved. "I was hoping you had seen them, though. I'm a little apprehensive about their situation, since only local police were involved so far."

"Is there anything I should do?"

"Only if you have the physical and emotional strength."

"If I don't, and something has happened to them, the trail will just get colder."

"I agree. Start just by asking if you can meet them. They may be frightened of you. See if Cori is willing."

"Geez. I hate to involve her."

Claris offered to help. "I'd like to chat with her anyway. Is now a good time?"

Stewart looked at Cori and held up the telephone. "Cori, do you want to talk to Claris?"

"Course." She picked up the telephone. "Hey V.I. Warshawski?"

"So glad to hear your voice, Jane Tenneson . . . or is it Brenda Leigh Johnson?"

"Touché!"

"How are you, really?"

"I'm getting there. Can't wait to be home, though."

"Granted. We can't wait to see you. Seriously Cori, very well done. Amazing. I know you hate praise, but thank you."

"You're right. Praise is hard to take. I don't know how else to do things!"

"Good thing. Stewart and I were discussing whether we should ask you for another favor. It's a biggie."

"Okay." Cori was cautious.

"Would you be willing to go with him to see if the other women who were abducted with Ava are really in the hotel? He figures, and I agree, that if they're not, we should be on it immediately."

"Yeah. I think we should get right on it. We'll let you know how it goes. Get help if you don't hear from us soon."

She said goodbye to Claris and was on her way to the door as she announced to the others, "Let's go!"

Ava wasn't sure what was going on. "You're leaving?"

Cori reassured her. "We're just going to see if the individuals you were taken with are really safe in the hotel."

"I'm coming too." Ava was off the bed and headed toward the door.

On their way to the lobby, using the stairs, Stewart made an observation that had crossed the minds of everyone. "We were never given keys to our room. Despite the reassurances, I'm still not feeling the freedom."

"Agreed." Cori chimed in.

Cori walked up to the counter. "We'd like individual keys for our room." She thought it was a good way to test the waters on the more important mission. She was surprised and relieved when the keys were produced.

"Ava would like reassurances that the people she was rescued with are okay. Could you please give us their room number?"

"That is a private matter." A very curt response.

Ava spoke this time. "I have their names, and I'm about to call the human rights watch organization."

Room 324.

"They're next door to us." Stewart stated the obvious, and they proceeded back upstairs.

Ava knocked on the door. She had picked up on a couple of phrases from her fellow captives that were intended for comforting one another. She called their names and one of the phrases she had heard.

One of the women opened the door. They embraced. Ava held up three fingers, using sign language to ask if everyone was accounted for.

The person at the door shook her head yes, and the other two emerged from the room and into the hallway to give Ava a hug.

Stewart at first kept his distance in the event a male presence would cause anxiety. Ava made a sign to inquire as to their well-being. She used the universal word, "Okay?" Stewart moved closer to her. She pointed to him and said, "He's okay." They glanced in his direction and they all repeated in unison, "Okay," and smiled.

They all said good night in English and went to their respective rooms. Once inside, Cori remarked on the encounter first. "I'm feeling a lot better about everything. Shall we try to get some sleep?"

She hadn't noticed that Stewart flew to Ava and had her check her pockets. He held his index finger to his lips, motioning folks to say nothing. Except he did. "Yeah, I've had it. Let's try to get a few hours of rest at least."

Ava continued to search her pockets while Stewart fetched the pad of paper and scribbled a note.

"Bug!"

Cori looked up from the note and held her hands palms up and shrugged her shoulders. Just about that time, Ava produced a tiny battery-like device. Stewart shook his head, "Yes."

Cori grabbed the note pad, "What's up?"

Steward explained as briefly as he could. "I could see that Ava didn't recognize one of the women, and one of them slipped something into her pocket. Ava put our tracker in the pocket of one she was sure was abducted."

"We're back where we started, and without a tracker!"

"Yup!"

"What should we do?"

He held up his hand as if to say, "Hold on," and dialed his cell. "Hi Claris. I just wanted to tell you we'll be resting for a while. If we're lucky, maybe they'll bring something other than poached eggs when we wake up. There's something missing in a meal like that. Have you heard anything new?"

Claris understood the code. If at any point someone started talking about food or the weather, she knew there were problems and needed to cue in on key words. "Things are good from this end. I hope you have a good rest, and we'll see you soon."

Stewart responded again with a code. "Yeah. It bugs me that we won't get to see the local sights and track what's going on, but I can't wait to get home at this point."

"Understood. Thanks. Sleep well." Claris got it. *Missing, local, track. Those are the clues.*

It took until the last exchange, but Cori and Ava understood that his call was code for the fact that they were bugged, the local police were corrupt, and he had given the GPS tracker to the others.

They watched him closely as he went around the room looking for any other bugs in the room. He found none.

Cori and Ava each took a bed. They realized he was going to keep an ear out for any movement next door. He heard shuffling about an hour after Cori and Ava fell asleep. He left them a note instructing them to trust embassy personnel since they had nothing else they could do but be sure to ask for credentials.

He waited a short time before exiting the room and rushed to catch up with the group that had been their neighbors. The darkness hid him well. He found a sleeping cab driver on the busy street outside of the hotel and decided to try following the perps.

The sleepy driver jumped into action. The driver and Stewart spotted the van at the same time, and the taxi driver pulled out after a reasonable length of time. Stewart gestured that he needed to make a phone call, and the driver quickly figured out that Stewart wanted a cell. He had left their only means of communication with Cori and Ava.

"Hey Claris. I'm in a cab and we're following a van that has two of the three women taken from the coal plant. We don't know who the third woman with them is. We think she's one of the perps. And we don't know where the third woman from the plant is."

"The bug?"

"Which one? I left theirs in the pocket of someone who was checking out at the hotel. I'm quite sure he was headed to the train. Ours is in the pocket of the captives."

Claris chuckled a bit. "I hope you didn't just get an innocent bystander killed or something. How are you calling?"

"Cab driver's phone."

"Okay, I wish you wouldn't follow them. Personnel from a U.S. passenger transit center in Europe, which is to remain unnamed, will arrive in the country soon. The airmen had been following the GPS, which activated motion a few minutes ago."

"Good. That's about right."

"I'll know when they stop, and . . .wait. I'm getting a call. I'll get back to you."

Stewart looked at the cab driver and motioned that it would be one more minute. The driver made a couple of quick turns. Despite the moderate speed, he let go of the wheel to make a motion like an airplane. Stewart surmised they were headed for the airport.

The cell rang. "Yup."

Claris rushed to tell him the U.S. airmen arrived at the airport and were confident that was where the GPS was headed.

"Are they prepared to ambush them?"

"In a manner of speaking. Everyone should be very careful because of the hostages."

"Of course." Stewart knew that all along, he just had to find some levity in the situation. "What about Cori and Ava?"

"The emissary should arrive by private plane soon. I hope it's not a perfect storm at that place. Everyone is arriving at once." Claris spoke quickly.

"Could be some donnybrook." Stewart said to himself, but it was audible to Claris.

"Outlandish!"

"This whole thing!"

"Should I get used to it?"

"I'd say! Gotta go. You'll hear from me." Stewart gave the cell back to the driver.

He motioned for the driver to stop on the perimeter of the airfield and asked him to stay put. Stewart exited the cab and jogged toward the small terminal in the shadows, never taking his sights off the van.

The van pulled up to the west side of a hangar. Stewart was unaware of any other activity at the small air strip. It stood in contrast to the conflagration he expected. He kept moving toward the terminal but stayed to the east since the van was facing west, almost out of his sight. He reached the outside walls of the terminal and started toward where the van was parked.

Abruptly he was stopped, and a hand cupped his mouth. No one spoke, but he saw at least four uniformed airmen. *How can I identify myself as an American with no ID? Especially with a hand over my mouth.* He had almost forgotten about a note he wrote in his pocket identifying himself and his situation. He motioned toward his pocket, and one of the servicemen checked it out. He nodded toward the man holding Stewart, and Stewart was released. No one spoke, though Stewart noted that these guys had the hand motions down to a science. He gathered there were others approaching from the opposite side of the terminal. Their aircraft must be hidden. *All we need now is for the Embassy envoy to arrive.*

No sooner had the thought formed than they heard an aircraft approaching. The group was forced to step up its action and were on the van in an instant. Two went directly to the driver's seat, two to the rear of the van, and four toward the aircraft. With the swiftness afforded by their training, they boarded, disarmed the guards, and apprehended the pilot. They dragged them out and tied them up, leaving them on the cold tarmac.

The three women were bound and gagged, but Stewart held the airmen back from freeing them. He needed to get a good look to be sure the fake captive wasn't poised to do lethal harm to a would-be liberator or worse, the whole group. He indicated which one should be left, and they hurried the other two women out of the van and put a good deal of distance between them and the van.

The aircraft they heard in the distance was just taxiing from what looked like a long cornfield. It stopped near their location, and several individuals deplaned.

One of the airmen approached them with his weapon at his side. He asked for identification, and all of them, three men and one woman, produced foreign service identification. One of the men verbally identified himself as Scott Perry and said he had been speaking with a Cori Sellers in China and Claris Sullivan stateside.

Stewart stepped forward. "I'm Stewart Montgomery." I'm here with Cori Sellers under a consulting agreement with Amity Associates, where Claris Sullivan serves in the Legal Department."

Perry looked at Stewart and then at the group. "I need a SITREP."

One of the airmen responded. "Five men have been apprehended by the security forces just moments ago. Three women were in the cargo portion of the van on the western side of the terminal. One is known to work with the abductors and is still in the van. A bomb squad will be called to ensure no explosives meant for law enforcement are present. The others are waiting for a taxi to the hotel. Sellers and another subject are waiting for your arrival at the hotel. There still is a missing hostage. Any update or plans you can tell me about?"

"The plane is being refueled, and half of our party will accompany Sellers, North, and Montgomery to Landstuhl for physical exams and then on to everyone's respective homes. The Chinese citizens will return to the U.S. Embassy in Beijing. The FBI will be on scene soon to begin the search for the missing girl and perhaps many more."

"The FBI?"

"An American citizen was one of the abductees. That immediately requires their involvement, though she now is accounted for. We are grateful for your involvement."

"It's not over. I won't be on that plane to Landstuhl."

"We'll talk."

"I need a big favor." Stewart was glad for the dimly lit tarmac because he was confident he showed signs of embarrassment. "I need money for the cab."

"Of course. Here is some currency for here, Germany, and home. Here also is a cellphone and an ID. Ask your friend the taxi driver if he can get a colleague to help ferry the remainder of us to the hotel."

Stewart paid the driver and made the request. The driver knew something very important was going on, and he was thrilled to be a part of the excitement. Stewart texted Claris.

"New cell. All is working out. The FBI on its way; airmen here and local authorities. Cori and Ava headed for safety soon. More later. Thanks, Stewart."

Two members of the envoy were security. The women and Perry went with the two hostages in the taxi. Stewart and the other two members of the envoy rode with his taxi driver. Local law enforcement officers were beginning to arrive, and the airmen stayed to secure the scene for the long haul, or however long it took for the FBI to arrive.

The local bomb squad arrived. They found a crude bomb attached to the bogus hostage. Luckily the detonator was not in her hand nor was it remote. It wasn't motion-sensitive either. Detonation would have required her hands to be free.

The taxis arrived at the hotel, and Stewart bounded up the stairs and knocked on the door to the room he had occupied with Cori and Ava. They looked out the peep hole, and immediately opened the door. The others arrived as well, and the room was soon crowded with the envoys and the two rescued hostages.

Stewart provided introductions where he could and asked those he didn't know to introduce themselves. He appointed himself to give an update, and one of the Embassy assistants translated for the Chinese citizens.

He then turned to Perry and implored, "Can we get these young women to their destinations now?"

"Yes. Let's."

Daylight was breaking as they drove into the terminal site. There seemed to be planes everywhere, unlike less than an hour ago when they departed for the hotel.

The FBI had arrived and had taken over the scene from the airmen and the local authorities. Stewart quickly ensured that he knew folk's names and he introduced himself to anyone new on the scene. He thanked whomever he thought provided or intended to provide help. A take-charge FBI agent directed Cori, Ava, and their envoys to the plane that was travelling to Landstuhl. She then directed the Chinese women and their envoys to the plane headed for Beijing, where they would receive any needed medical attention, debriefing and questioning, and compensation for their time.

When the separate planes were ready for take-off, Lani Richards, the take-charge agent, approached Stewart. "Mr. Montgomery, we need you on the plane to Landstuhl now please."

"I'm staying to help."

"We can't have you do that."

"I insist. I am a freelance extractor and a licensed PI."

"Thank you for your service, but we can't use you for this mission."

"Agent Richards, I really need to be a part of this."

"We've got it."

"Don't get me wrong, I am indebted to you and anyone responsible for your involvement, but I need 'in.'"

"Here's the best I can do. Accompany the Chinese citizens back to Beijing and help with the debriefing. You can be checked out as well and stay courtesy of the Embassy. Or, you can travel with Ms. Sellers and Ms. North."

Stewart was not torn between the options. He was confident that Cori and Ava were in good hands. "Thanks. Beijing it is."

He went by Cori's plane and said goodbye. "I have your cell numbers, and I'll be in touch. You do the same." He thought he saw tears in Cori's eyes, but he was stone-cold in his decision to stay with this case.

He deplaned and boarded the Embassy plane. They idled while letting the plane Cori was on take-off first.

Chapter 19

Cori and Ava agreed there was plenty of room to stretch out, so they sat in different rows. A sandwich platter was available. It wasn't breakfast food, but they were ravenous and didn't care. They had enough poached eggs as it was.

Cori didn't know whether texting was allowed on the plane. She would have asked permission, but she felt too tired. There had been no contact with Roman or Micah for so long. She wondered if they were worried. *Claris kept them informed, I'm sure. I wouldn't have wanted that responsibility. I don't know what I would say had I updated them at intervals during the last few days.*

Cori looked over at Ava, who was sleeping. That's what Cori wanted. A long, peaceful sleep. She was grateful to be safe and comfortable. The fatigue was so overwhelming that she wasn't even sure she could utter a prayer of thanks. And, she was worried. *Why am I worried? I am too tired. I can't think. Something is missing*. An image of Stewart came to memory. *Stewart went to China. He's not with us. This isn't over.* Then she slept.

She felt the plane touch down. It took almost as long to wake up fully as for the plane to taxi to a stop. Ava stirred long after Cori was fully awake. "I think we're here."

Ava was groggy and mumbled, "Okay. Good."

They were surprised to be met by ambulances, and they were whisked away to the hospital. Warm blankets, X-rays, blood tests, CT scans, questions from nurses, questions from doctors, questions from psychologists. Amid it all, Cori couldn't help but think that she saw very few uniforms given that it was an army medical center. During a break in the probing and prodding, Cori decided it was time to make some calls. *Have I been avoiding them?* She asked one of the technicians who was checking the leads to her heart monitor if her cell would work. He asked if it was Tri-Band.

"I'm not sure about this one since it was given to me."

"I'll look at the SIM card. Why don't you use one of the hospital lines? Mention it to the psychologist. She'll make it part of your plan."

Cori thought her answer was a little sketchy, but she was beginning to desire what she had been avoiding. Eventually her nurse appeared, and she asked her about telephone calls to the States.

"You mean you haven't called home? Of course. The telephone in your room can be used. It's important not to overdo it, but most everyone has two or three key people they need to contact. Especially given what you've been through. I'll give you some privacy. In the meantime, give me your cell, and I'll check out the SIM card." He took the telephone and left the room.

Cori got a line from the operator, and then dialed Roman. Luckily, she remembered his cell.

"Hello?" He sounded suspicious. No surprise. She wasn't sure how this showed up on caller ID.

"It's Cori."

"Cori! Thank God I answered! The caller ID said Germany! Where are you? How are you?"

"Germany! Good. How much else do you know so I won't bore you?"

"Claris called yesterday to say you had encountered problems but were okay."

"She hadn't called before then?"

"No. I was sure we would have heard something from you, even though I don't know that much about calls from overseas. What happened?"

"Remember, I'm safe. I'm at Landstuhl Army Medical Center *just as a precaution*." She emphasized the last four words. She gave as brief a summary as she could and explained she should be back at home in a couple of days. "Roman, how are you?"

"Floored. I can't believe what you just said."

"I know. I'm sorry to rush you, but I shouldn't make it a long call. So, how are you?"

"I'm home again. Helen was able to get an apartment, and Ainsleigh is recuperating well with her parents. I'm up and able to heat up meals and take care of myself quite well. Respiratory comes in once a day and nursing twice a day. But I'm lonely. Sorry. How can I complain after your last few days?"

"I'd complain all of the time if I were you. I'm so sorry. When can Ainsleigh come home?"

"I think soon."

"Good. I might not call again until I'm in the States. Try not to worry."

"Thanks for calling. Good to hear your voice."

"You too. For sure."

Poor Roman. If only Ainsleigh could be there.

She asked for another line and dialed Claris. She realized she had no idea what time it was in Arizona nor at home. She let the call go through anyway.

It was voicemail. Cori understood why Claris might need some sleep after being their point person 24/7. She left a message and said she would call back later. Impulsively, she called Micah.

"Micah Flores."

"Micah. It's Cori."

"Cori. It's good to hear from you. How are you? The caller ID said Germany." He chuckled nervously.

"I am in Germany. Just as a precaution, I am at Landstuhl Army Medical Center."

"What? Why?"

"This is a little of what happened." She proceeded to tell him as little as possible, but she was truthful.

"That is unbelievable." After a long pause, "Really, it is. But I'm glad you're safe. When can you come home?"

"I think in a couple of days. I'll let you know more then."

"Promise you'll call as soon as you're home?"

"Promise."

"Thanks so much for calling."

"You're welcome."

"I miss you."

"I miss you too."

She was a little shaken by the call because she didn't know how she felt about Micah. She obviously wanted to talk to him. She wasn't overtly angry at him. He was strong, kind and attractive. She was confused by her conflicted feelings.

But it was time to try Claris again.

"Claris."

"Hey Claris. If I were to mimic Lucy mimicking Ricky Ricardo, I'd say, 'You have some splainin' to do!'"

"Cori. It's good to hear from you, I think! What are you talking about?"

"Stewart! Working for Amity. Traveling with me! Not to mention his role in your unspoken enterprise!" It was a high-pitched statement.

"I only knew the truth about Stewart when I was approached about the task force on human trafficking. If you had accepted a role on the team, I would have told you before you found out some other way. I didn't know he was on his way to China with you until you left town, but you didn't get back to me when I texted. Trust me on this. I trust you with a lot of confidential information. I would have trusted you with this information if it wasn't 'need to know.'"

There was no comment.

"Cori."

"Ah, leave me alone. I want to be mad, but how can I? You make too much sense. And we would be dead or worse if it wasn't for you."

"Then you're not angry."

"No. I am thankful. I'm worried about Stewart and the hostage they haven't found."

"We all are. I wish I could be there."

"Me too. Not! You're right where you should be!"

Claris smirked, and somehow Cori could tell and closed the conversation. "I'll get my sense of adventure back. I think."

Despite Cori's broken ribs, which she admitted were sore but tolerable, Ava and Cori were cleared medically. Psych services expressed concern that they hadn't processed the trauma. Ava provided the explanation that worked for her. "I'm still in survival mode. I think I will be until I reach home. Who knows what I will be like when I'm finally surrounded by friends and family."

Cori agreed. "How can normality return until normality returns? Please don't try to assess us accurately under the circumstances. We're thankful to be here. Thank you for your care. We just want to go home."

They were released toward the middle of the day, and their flight wasn't until the following morning. One of the hospital volunteers asked if they would like to see some of the surrounding sites. Physically they were fine, but it was difficult to garner interest in tourist attractions. They knew they would regret it if they passed on the opportunity, so they graciously accepted.

Cori and Ava discussed the little they knew about the area. Often, they had heard about seriously wounded service personnel medevacked from Iraq and Afghanistan to nearby Ramstein Air Base for treatment at LRMC. They admitted to the volunteer, Stella, that they would leave it up to her to decide what was interesting for them to see.

"I think the view from Nanstein Castle is breathtaking, and I am really impressed with the interesting history they cover. The Castle dates to the twelfth century and fell into disrepair after the Knights Revolt in 1523. It was restored a few years later and then the fortifications were razed in 1668. But you'll hear all of that and more if you would like to go? There's a nice German restaurant close by where we can have an early dinner before you return to your hotel. Sound okay?"

It really did, and they had a wonderful time. It was all she said it would be and more. Stella was a wonderful guide, interpreter, and foodie. As they studied the menu prior to dinner, they realized their knowledge of German cuisine was superficial at best. Stella was ready with suggestions—Schweinshaxe or Schnitzel if they were in the mood for meat and veggies, or Doner if they were hankering for a sandwich.

"Can you elaborate?" Cori asked, and they all chuckled.

Schnitzel varies a lot, but it is great here. It is thinned veal that is breaded and served with veggies and a hollandaise sauce. Schweinshaxe is ham hocks and very delicious. Doner is a bread pocket filled with your choice of pork or chicken and stuffed with shredded cabbage, carrots, and other yummy ingredients."

Ava was on her toes and suggested they order one of each and do a little sharing. They enjoyed every bite and though they were stuffed, they shared a serving of Black Forest Gateau (Schwarzwalder Kirschtorte on the menu) for dessert.

Stella had a final suggestion when she dropped them off at their hotel. "Be sure to have a Berliner for breakfast. This hotel serves them free."

"Thanks for everything Stella."

"I had fun. You take care of yourselves."

They each had a Berliner the next morning and agreed that it was as good as any donut they had ever eaten.

Ava chose to fly into Newark with Cori. She was from a small town in Pennsylvania, and her family met her at the airport. Cori was introduced to Ava's mom and brother. They chatted for a short time and then made haste to finish the last legs of their long journey.

*   *   *

Cori didn't call anyone to say she was in the States, she just drove home. As she did, the awesome feeling that freedom brings washed over her. Simply driving her own car was an overwhelming privilege she had regarded as an entitlement. With thankfulness always came an awareness of the way things might not be and those who were not free from the constraints imposed on them by others.

Myriad roles of captors raced through her mind. Men and women who, in their own households, exercised control over the bodies and/or minds of those with whom they lived and loved. Individuals who lured others into their control through the promise of love, money, a new land, or whatever opportunity might appeal. Powerful leaders who convince their subordinates of harm that will come to them by refusing to participate in immoral or illegal practices. The unprecedented numbers of people of faith whose freedoms were stripped from them based only on their faith perhaps was the most underreported and least understood in this whole arena. It was amazing to her that folks could be so threatened by ideas of faith and practices of worship alone. She said a quick prayer of thanks for her freedom and for all who lived in the shadows.

She was finally home. Her car was in the carport. She was in her condo. Her messy condo. Her mess. She could clean it up, or she could ignore it. She could starve or could get some food. Freedom.

It was time to make some calls. She called Roman first, who was as enthusiastic about her arrival as she had seen him about anything since his wedding. She felt guilty about resenting him over the comments he made to Byron. It hadn't changed her love for him, but she allowed it to erode her appreciation of their relationship and the qualities of character he possessed in large quantities.

She called Claris and Jessalyn. Jessalyn knew nothing of what was going on, so they arranged to have an early supper before Jessalyn's overnight shift. She called Micah. For a short time in their relationship, he would have been first.

"Micah Flores."

"Hi. It's Cori. I wanted to let you know I'm home. Happy to be home!"

"Good. Very good in fact. Can we get together?"

If I tell him I'm having supper with a girlfriend, he'll know he was down the list of callers.

"Of course. What's good?"

"I'm about to leave Boston. I won't be in town for a few hours, and I really need to make an appearance at the Landing. Dinner is out. How about a late dessert?"

"That works." Cori didn't show her relief.

"Same place?"

"Sure."

"Is nine o'clock too late?"

"That's fine. See you then."

"I can't wait. Bye."

"Bye."

She had time to shop for a new cell and a few items of clothing she would miss most until hers arrived from Xi'an—if they

ever appeared. She was at the Sandwich Shop ahead of Jessalyn.
She wanted to call Stewart. All along she wanted to call Stewart.
She finally summoned the nerve and dialed the cell phone provided to him by the Beijing Embassy. He answered on the first
ring.

"Montgomery."

It was him. He repeated his greeting, the pause was so long.

"It's Cori."

"Finally. Are you home and safe?"

"Yes."

"Good. How did it go?"

"We were well-cared for. I just arrived at my condo this afternoon. I met Ava's family in Newark. They're nice. But how about
you? What's going on?"

"They kept me in the hospital until today. They said my head
wound warranted it. I think they just wanted to keep me out of
the fray. I'm in a taxi and on my way to the Embassy to check
out what's going on."

"Are you sure you're feeling okay? No concussions or
anything?"

"Nope. No headaches, infections, or anything. Just lucky."

"Why don't you just come back to the States?"

There was a long pause. "I probably might as well. The trail
is cold by now, and the FBI is not going to include me. I should
have traveled with you and Ava."

"Then come."

"I'll let you know."

"Good. Call me."

"Yup." The typical Stewart would have teased her about missing him and wanting him back in the States. But it hurt a little too much to think of her back in Laurel Ledge with Micah.

* * *

Stewart wasn't out of clues entirely. And coming to Beijing was an okay perch for what he had planned, which was to fly to Xi'an first. He wasn't finished with the energy plant. There were more involved from the plant, and he didn't trust the authorities to follow through. *Hell, were most of them involved?* He just had to hope that the FBI would find the missing women.

The English-speaking clerk was surprised to see him when he walked up to the registration desk at the Hilton Hotel in Xi'an. "Mr. Montgomery. Good to see you again. You want a room?"

"Yes."

"How many days?"

"Uh, I don't know. Is that okay?"

"Yes. That's okay."

The hotel wasn't busy. She gave him the same room he stayed in a few days ago. She also acted as the concierge and arranged for a rental car. Just as he was about to leave the hotel, he swung around and inquired of Neil. She answered quickly, "He left." She looked at her computer. "Three days ago."

"Thanks," Stewart replied as he was swiftly out the door. He was a little despondent not to have a cohort, though it was better not to have any responsibilities for someone else's safety. He headed out to the plant alone. He found Bao sitting as his desk, staring straight ahead.

Stewart knocked so Bao wouldn't be as startled by his approach. Bao swung around and looked as though the zombie apocalypse was upon him.

"Hey Bao. How are things?"

Bao only spoke a few words of English. He still looked frightened and held his defensive position.

Why didn't I bring an interpreter?

Stewart tried to communicate and keep Bao calm at the same time. "It's okay. Is the plant still running?"

Bao seemed to understand. "A little longer."

They're probably running it just long enough to get customers set up with other suppliers.

"Are you looking for a job?"

"Need a job, yes."

"You're here."

"Yes. Work for now."

"Is there someone who speaks English?"

"Engineer."

"Can we get him?" Stewart gestured more than talked.

Bao led him out of the office and into another wing of the run-down plant that Stewart hadn't seen before. He was the sole other worker in that room. Definitely a skeleton crew. Bao did his best to introduce them. "Stewart, Li Jie."

"Thanks, Bao. Stay please," with gestures.

"Jie, may I call you Jie?" Stewart tried to be courteous because he was about to ask several favors.

"Yes."

"Do you know I was here the other day?"

"Yes. That's the reason the plant is closing."

Stewart tried not to scoff. "Do you know what was going on?"

"Yes."

"Did you know?"

"No. It's terrible. But I don't know why we have to lose our jobs."

"Look, I hope you can get jobs other places. Do you know who was involved?"

"We think we know. They were the only ones who didn't show up for work the next day. We were so ignorant."

"Do you know their names?"

"Yes. We gave them to the authorities."

"Would you write down the names for me?"

"Sure," and Jie proceeded to do so.

"Do you think anything will be done?" Stewart asked while Jie was still writing. When Jie was finished, he handed the names to Stewart along with other papers without mentioning the contents. He only answered Stewart's question.

"Yes. The owners will make sure. They're p***ed."

Stewart almost chuckled with a snort but stifled it just in time.

"Were there authorities involved too?"

"Probably not. They just don't care. They want to catch people who steal *things*, not women."

Most of the world thinks that way, unfortunately. Even in the United States.

"Thanks. I had to know, and I'm sorry about your jobs. I'm glad you're safe, though. These people tried to kill me."

"Yes. We know."

Stewart shook hands with them. He hoped Jie was right about the owners' intent to find the perpetrators and have them prosecuted. Otherwise, they could set up shop again just about anywhere.

Stewart returned to the hotel and told them he would be checking out the following day. He obtained a visa for Kazakhstan while in Beijing, but after reviewing the documents Jie slipped to him, he knew it was more important to travel to Uzbekistan. He booked flights to Almaty and Tashkent for the next day. He told the Embassy in Beijing what he had heard at the old plant and the names of the owners. He asked about a visa for Uzbekistan, and they told him it would be available in Almaty.

He called Amnesty International and asked how to make a report. They told him a detailed email would do, and he spent the rest of the day documenting everything he could about the facts surrounding the old plant and his experiences with Cori and Ava. He gave them permission to share the information wherever it would be helpful, and he alerted them to his plans in Uzbekistan.

The hard thing about this lousy business is every time you alert someone it could be another player abetting the operation. He still suspected the local police, there had to be an engineer involved at the plant, maybe one of the owners, and he wasn't completely trusting that individuals with the hotel and even the Embassy hadn't benefitted from the operation in some way. He didn't suspect Amnesty International.

* * *

Cori remained at the Sandwich Club after her quick supper with Jessalyn. She was still hungry; she and Jessalyn did some girlfriend power talking to process all that had happened. Jessalyn had seen human misery as a nurse, but she was shocked by Cori's personal account of the disregard for human freedom. *What a gem she is. Jessalyn is kind, wise, and a source of support I don't get from many people.*

Cori was deep in thought and became aware of a shadow standing over her. Almost at the same moment she heard, "Hi Cori. I hope you haven't waited long."

She sprang to her feet and hugged Micah. It was marvelous being in his arms again, and, for the moment, she wondered what the resentment had been about. He didn't move to kiss her, though, and they sat down beside each other on the bench. They remained touching as if drawing strength and comfort from the closeness.

He spoke first. "Tell me everything."

So, she did. She was glad she had ventured into a review of the scary details first with Jessalyn. Rather than falling apart, she was able to remain composed while telling Micah. Micah had seen a great deal of seediness during his life and career, much like Jessalyn, yet in different ways. Despite his experience, he, like Jessalyn, was shaken.

"I want to do anything I can to help you. I feel responsible."

Cori was abrupt. "There wasn't anything you could do! Don't feel responsible."

"I guess I know that. It's just in the DNA." He was abjectly sad. "I also know I sent you off to that horrible experience with a bad feeling. I want to make that right."

Cori was silent. Her job was to help people sort out the emotional quagmires encountered in life, but she hated doing it with people who were close to her. *I think I'm a terminal hypocrite.* She, like everyone, wanted people who supposedly cared to figure it out for themselves.

His voice showed that he was still upset. "I know it was about your involvement with Roman. I think I gave you the 'B' answer."

"I suppose that did nothing but reinforce what an awful person I am." She was a little humbler than their previous conversation, for the moment. "Here's what I meant. Everyone assumed that all my comments were about me. Could it be possible that all along my concern was about what was best for Roman? That the years of caring for him amassed knowledge that can't be gleaned from charts, and experts, and research?"

Then her intensity increased. "All this talk about, 'you're free now, Cori,' 'it's not up to you now, Cori,' 'they need their space now, Cori,' 'they're happy the way they are, Cori.' At the end of the day, when his health is in especial peril, I think I need to be there! What is so bleeping hard about that!"

Sheepish wasn't the word. "Nothing." He knew this was going off the rails.

"Probably you've had enough of me for right now. Thanks for listening. Let me know if you recover and see any point in continuing our friendship."

"There is nothing that would prompt me to throw away our friendship, Cori. You have a point of view, and I'm sorry I trampled all over your feelings. I think I've learned a lot about you. I appreciate it."

"Most men would have walked away."

"Please tell me we're not giving up."

"No. We're not giving up."

"Do you feel like some dessert?"

"Actually, I'm starved. I think I want dinner!"

Eventually the mood lightened a bit, and they had an enjoyable dinner as friends.

Chapter 20

Amity was generous in offering consultants R & R after travel. Especially given what Cori had been through. After a couple of days of household chores, which were no fun with a broken rib, she was ready for work. Travel was not on the docket for at least the first week after her return. Most of her assignments were through email, video calls, or written work.

She and Micah went to a concert in Hartford, saw a movie, and did some work together at the Landing. He was following her lead, and her feelings of trust and affection for him were rebuilding. They returned from a late dinner one night, and he walked her to her condo door.

"I know we weren't together long before your China experience, but I've missed the closeness. Would you object to a kiss tonight?"

"No."

He kissed her, gently.

"How about more?"

Her voice quaked a bit even as she softly answered, "Sure."

The kiss was still gentle, but long. He stopped for a moment and looked into her eyes as if to say it was about to become intense. It did. There was desire, excitement. For the first time, their open mouths were one, exploring, probing, increasing the hunger felt throughout their bodies. Their breathing and soft moans mirrored the other's rising physical responses.

The hunger for each other continued for some time, but eventually Micah slowly released her lips. The way he did it was sexy. She let go of his reluctantly. He squeezed her in a tight embrace and barely voiced the words, "I think I'd better say goodnight. As much as I hate to."

"I know. Thank you, Micah, for a lovely evening and for putting up with me. I know I'm a handful."

"An exciting, exotic handful." He turned and left.

He is so special. How could I have treated him so badly. He doesn't deserve me. He deserves someone so much better.

He was special. He was attractive and kind. He seemed into her, but she didn't know why. Still she sensed he didn't "get" her in the way she thought she wanted. *Maybe he accepts the disconnect as mysteriously exciting. If he's just overlooking it to placate me, that's not okay.*

Chapter 21

Stewart deplaned in Tashkent not sure what he was going to do. He used some of the USD wired from his service in the States to exchange for Uzbekistani so'm currency, UZS, at the airport. He understood the possibility that the hostages were ferried off to another country, but he wanted to be prepared for staying in Uzbekistan if necessary. Typically, he posed as a prospective customer while investigating details for a planned extraction.

He was staring around the terminal to clear his mind and develop a plan when his cell phone rang. It wasn't a number already in his phone, but he had only inputted emergency numbers in the cell given to him by the Embassy.

"Montgomery."

"It's Li Jie. Engineer."

"Oh. Hey. I didn't expect to hear from you."

"I found something. It might be an address. It looks Russian."

"Do you have a cell that can send a text and picture out of the country."

"Powerful. Yes. Best on the market. I'm an engineer."

"Yes. And a good investigator, and just a darn good person, too. Can you take a picture and text it to me?"

"Yes." Jie's statements were deadpan. He was interesting, to say the least. Stewart sensed Jie didn't care for him, but the man must be overcoming his bad feelings to do the right thing.

"How did you get my number?"

"Hotel."

"Thanks. I'll let you know how things go."

"I'll call. Delete my number for now."

A wise request.

"Sure." He received the address, and he took a chance that it was in Tashkent. He grabbed a cab and showed the driver the address.

The driver scowled. He held up his hands and rubbed his fingers and thumbs in a circular motion. *A universal gesture.* Stewart handed him 100,000 so'm, generous fare according to Stewart's research. The driver shook his head that it wasn't enough. He handed him 50,000 so'm, and the driver still refused to drive. Stewart retrieved the money from the driver's open palm and began to exit the taxi. The driver gestured by opening and closing his hand frantically and raised his voice. "Okay, okay." He put the 50,000-note into the cash box and pocketed the other while steering the rattle trap of a car into traffic.

It was a long ride, and the roads became rough. It was obvious they were outside of the city limits. Stewart knew the trip was prolonged intentionally, not so much to increase the fare but likely to keep Stewart from remembering the directions. He would remember. Unwittingly the driver helped by passing a hospital on the way.

Stewart couldn't allow himself to lose focus on what he was here to do, but he thought about the research that informed him on these former Soviet countries. Under different circumstances, he wanted to understand the rich histories, the art, and the distinct architecture. He was curious about the Silk Road, with Tashkent squarely in the center of the ancient route that spanned 7,000 miles from China to Western Turkey. He wanted to see the historic settlements, palaces, temples, and tombs that were World Heritage sites as well as the breathtaking mountains and lakes. He had gotten a glimpse of the turquoise domes and ancient buildings as the taxi wended its way out of Tashkent.

Their final turn was on a short, dead-end street. The driver nearly took Stewart's foot with him when he drove off. Stewart surmised the driver knew what the address represented and didn't want to have his cab associated with delivering Stewart to the premises.

Stewart wasn't armed, and he didn't have much of a plan. He had texted a picture of the address to a group he had set up—Claris, Trent, embassies in Beijing, Almaty, and Tashkent, but wasn't sure what good it would do.

At first glance, the windows looked like any other house but were blocked by mirror material. All he saw was his own reflection. The building had dilapidated shingle siding. It was a detached building, and there were a few neighboring buildings in no better condition. Stewart decided to watch and see what he could learn about the area and its activities. Over a period of an hour or more, no one passed by on the sidewalk, entered, nor left any of the buildings on the street. No cars passed by. At least, he hadn't seen or heard any.

He walked around the house and found a couple of pieces of siding hanging from the building. With a little help, they were completely removed. He could see no one from where he stood, and he was sure no one could see him. So, he proceeded to remove building materials. There was little insulation, some lath and plaster, which he assumed was the last layer. He worked at it gradually with his pocket knife trying to whittle away a little at a time. If the house was mice-infested, and likely it was, no one would think anything of the scraping noise.

It was cold out, but luckily there was no wind. He hoped no one would notice the draft created by the hole. The jagged opening was tiny, but it didn't take much space to crawl through. Once inside, he looked around to see if anyone might be watching. It was dark. He stayed low and tried to adjust to what he was seeing. It seemed like a dining room of sorts. It was so filthy no one would want to eat there. He still hadn't seen anyone.

He stayed low and crawled past the kitchen area. It was used, but not at the moment. He continued low, against the wall, until he came to a hall. There were several open doors; unlikely where prisoners would be held. There was a closed door. He tried to open it, but it was locked. He picked the lock as quietly as he could and opened it slowly.

There was nothing but darkness. He suspected stairs, and the musty smell supported his hunch. He used the flashlight from his cell for just a second to be positive. He descended the stairs on his bottom for no apparent reason. He shined the light briefly at the bottom. He saw no one, but he could hear muffled sounds. He waited for his eyes to adjust and saw a door. He moved closer to the door and the sounds became a bit louder. The door was locked, and he tried to pick it as before. It worked, and he opened the door.

He hoped eventually, if he lived long enough, he would forget the scene in front of him. He couldn't count the number of very young women in the squalor of the room. He was amazed they were silent. He closed the door behind him and shined his light at the ceiling. He called the only name he knew, provided by Ava. "Xiong Fa? Xiong Fa? Ava sent me."

Still there was silence. He waited. There was no doubt he had been heard.

A quiet voice next to him startled him. "Xiong Fa."

He handed her the cell, and she could see her picture and Ava's. She stood up. She spoke very little English, but said, "Ava. Friend?"

"Yes, friend."

Whatever she said to the other women was effective. He opened the door, shined the light, and they proceeded up the stairs. Many had little or no clothing, so, in a frenzy, he pulled down drapes, and gathered the table cloth and any towels he could locate. He took off his coat and shirt, and they went out on the street.

The bizarre group started walking toward the hospital, which was just a half dozen blocks away. He didn't have an eidetic memory, but it was almost always accurate. No cars were in sight, but they had been only a few blocks when a police car descended on them and came to screeching halt. Then another appeared and a third. Yelling police exploded from the cars and quickly grabbed Stewart and cuffed him. He had little time to think, but the emotional smack down was worse than the punches leveled at him as they crammed him into the back of one of the "cruisers." The women were forced into the other two police vehicles.

Stewart was socked around a bit more once in the police station, even though he hadn't resisted or said a word. He didn't know where they had taken the women. There were no attempts to question him. He was hauled out of the cruiser, given a couple of courtesy punches in the gut as he was shoved into a cell, still in cuffs.

After hours in isolation, someone came through the metal door whom he recognized even in the darkness. It was Lani Richards from the FBI. She didn't greet him, but simply motioned towards him and the guards who accompanied her through the door. He stepped out, and the cuffs were removed. He rubbed his wrists and followed Lani out into the lobby.

She exited the building, so he followed her there, too. Once outside, he broke the silence. "How are the women?"

"We got 'em. There were ten." She continued walking toward a cab and got in. He did too.

They arrived at the airport still in icy silence and immediately boarded a plane. No stop at a ticket counter or a venture through customs. Once on the plane, Stewart saw a group of women, some of whom looked familiar. One was Xiong Fa. They all were dressed in clean, warm clothing. When he came into full view, there was spontaneous applause, sustained over quite a long period. He smiled sheepishly and nodded. "You did it. You made it."

"Mr. Montgomery, we would like to take off. Please take a seat and fasten your seatbelt." Ms. Richards sounded gruff and impatient.

They were served cold sandwiches, hot coffee and ice water. He was ravenous but fell asleep before he could finish his meal. When he awakened, his meal had been cleared away. They still were traveling in silence. It was uncharacteristic of him to go along with the crowd, but in this instance, he did.

He was still basking in the knowledge that ten women were no longer in bondage. He knew Richards was miffed with him, and he cared not a bit. In this situation, the silent treatment was a hoot. He was seldom bothered by it anyway. He could only think of one person from whom the silent treatment would hurt.

Hours of travel finally ended. He guessed they had landed in Germany to be treated at Landstuhl. Ambulances arrived, and the plan appeared for them all to be taken on stretchers. Stewart refused, not so gently. Not surprisingly, the women complied.

Stewart succumbed to wearing a hospital johnny and occupying a bed. He was about to start notifying folks of his safety when Lani Richards entered his room and loomed over him.

"What were you thinking Montgomery?"

"Only a moment at a time."

"You could face charges."

He was determined to hold his anger after such a victory, but he couldn't help it. "Give it all you've got if that's what you want. Those women are free, and I can live on that the rest of my life. For now, let's just say I was working for the family of Xiong Fa to free their daughter."

"It could have turned out disastrous for them and you. You could have waited for us."

"And I would have if I had heard one word from you and knew what the devil was going on. Two-way street! This is what I do. If you want to lock me up for it, go right ahead. And you're welcome. I think I'm supposed to be resting, unless this is part of the debriefing."

She turned to leave, and he called out to her.

"There's a leak. I think I know who it is."

Chapter 22

Stewart didn't intend to stay in the hospital. His only reason for hanging around at all was to get the full story on what would happen to the women. Knowing how unlikely it was for information to be shared with him, he got impatient. He was an extractor, and that's all he set out to do.

He passed the time by making his intended calls. "Claris, it's Stewart. What's up?"

"What's up with you is the question?"

"What do you know?"

"That in a cowboy act you freed ten women, including Xiong Fa. So?"

"It's true. I'm at Landstuhl, and I think they're still here too. We flew here together, but apart from applause when I boarded the plane, and a quick observation that they all had on weather-appropriate garments, I haven't heard a word from them or about them. I don't think Richards is going to tell me anything. She's steamed."

"She has to pretend."

"I don't think she knows how. What else have you heard? You probably know more than I do."

"It's tricky. They don't intend to hold the women against their will since that's an affront to what they've been through. They plan to question any that are willing and certainly offer as much treatment as they will accept in the setting of their choice, after they're cleared medically. They will be provided transportation to wherever they choose to go."

"Do you know who they are?"

"Four or five were from the plant. Apparently, they were recruited as migrant workers with the promise of a salary and training at the university. They were forced to send postcards to their parents so that no one would question what happened to them.

"The FBI had the house staked and apprehended two perps. We're thankful the police didn't warn them first. They weren't going to release you, by the way. I suspect the intent to return the girls to the captors was in the works until they realized the extent of the flares you sent out. The rest of the cell in Uzbekistan remains unknown.

"The owners of the plant saw to it that the employees involved were arrested. But, I think the U.S. is going to try to take jurisdiction because an American was abducted. Trent and I aren't prepared to work on international law yet, so I can't comment on that. In fact, we haven't gotten to our domestic training because of this case. Ahem!" She cleared her throat knowing he would get her meaning.

"The legal maneuvers could take time. It's even more difficult with Uzbekistan than with other countries, I understand."
Claris finally wrapped up the report.

"I'm glad you're on it. Thanks for the info. I'm checking out
of here if I'm not under arrest, and I'll be home soon."

"You're not under arrest." Claris was emphatic and a little
mocking in her tone.

"Good." Stewart was in good humor, finally. "I don't know if
Richards cared about the crumb I left her, but the Uzbeks were
tipped off. There's no other explanation for how they snatched
us up so quickly."

"Any ideas."

"Ideas, yes. Proof, no."

"Want to share?"

"The head of the project, Neil."

Chapter 23

Cori and Micah were enjoying a burger at a fast-food restaurant when Claris called. "I spoke with Stewart. He's okay."

Cori had heard the account of the rescue near Tashkent from Claris the day before, though she was skeptical of his safety until someone heard from him directly. She was relieved, and it was apparent in her voice. "Oh good. When is he coming home?"

"As soon as he can, even if it has to be AMA!"

"I know how he feels."

"Don't be surprised if you hear from him. He was asking about you."

"I hope I do. Thanks!"

Micah could deduce what it was about. "The renegade Stewart has been found?"

"He has. Claris heard from him. What a relief!"

"He's a hero, I guess. I'm jealous." Micah smirked.

"You are a hero, every day. I didn't know that status was important to you, though." Cori was genuine but jovial.

"It's not the hero part that I'm jealous of." He looked at her in a teasing manner.

"Stop!" She was smiling as she said it, and she stole one of his fries in a gesture of punishment that was more like a gesture of intimacy.

* * *

Cori was still in the no-travel time for work but was fully engaged in full days at the office writing curriculum for new trainees hired in the wake of "Me Too." The volunteer work she had been promising to benefit the Landing was underway as well. She hadn't seen Della since their Sunday lunch with Micah right after the first of the year, and she very much wanted to see her and the other girls. She texted Reina, and they agreed on a time. It was Della's role to invite the other girls.

The girls, four in all, got off the bus at her condo after school later that week. Each had remembered their permission notes from their families. They made valentine cards for residents in the local healthcare center, and they intended to deliver them the following week. They were preparing pizzarettes, Cori's mini-pizza invention using toasted English muffins, red sauce, mozzarella, and the toppings of one's choice, for a quick supper.

In the middle of their preparations, the doorbell rang. Cori was stunned to see Stewart at the door. Despite the presence of the girls, she cried his name, and grabbed him in a quick embrace. "It's really you! How did you find me?"

She realized what she had said and held her hand over her mouth and giggled. "I forgot with whom I was dealing for a moment. Come in. Have supper with us."

After stepping inside, he noticed the girls working away at the island, which separated the kitchen area from the dining area. "Oh, I don't want to interrupt your party!"

"Nonsense. It'll be more of a party. Girls, this is my friend, Mr. Montgomery."

"Stewart." He interjected.

In the manner characteristic of these enthusiastic girls, they announced in unison, "Hi, Mr. Montgomery!"

Stewart leaned forward a bit from the waist and gently repeated, "Stewart."

Just as enthusiastically they squealed, "Stewart!"

"That's better. Now, who are all of you?"

"We're friends. Sometimes we have a GNO. But tonight, we're stayin' in!"

"I can see that."

"We're going to make some for you. We'll let you do the toppings."

Cori invited him to sit on the sofa, and she sat adjacent to him in the club chair. "When did you get back?"

"I just flew in. This was my first stop. I wanted to see how you are." Stewart wasn't going to hide his concern.

"How I am. How are you?" Cori emphasized the last word.

"I'm good. In a case like this, I don't think you can expect a better outcome." There was relief in his tone.

"True."

"Thanks for your help. You were the lynchpin that made it all possible."

"Not so true.

"I really came because I can smell the pizza and I'm hungry." He found a way once again to lighten the mood.

The girls overheard every word. "Then let's get this show on the road!" Louise was a faithful spokesperson for her friends.

"Let's!" Stewart jumped up from the sofa, asked which ones they had prepared for him. "I'm going to make a margherita pizza."

"Yikes!" Louise spoke up again. "Won't that be kinda' soggy?"

Della to the rescue. "It's a kind of pizza, not a drink. I think we have basil right here, but no sun-dried tomatoes."

In no time, they were eating their delicacies.

"Hey, these are good!" Louise was the only one to speak. The rest were too busy to form a word. They all just gave their various versions of, "Mmmm!"

Chewing wasn't a deterrent to Louise. She decided to tell jokes. Stewart was her target.

"Knock, knock."

Stewart was a sport. "Who's there?"

"A broken pencil."

"A broken pencil, who?"

"Never mind. It's pointless."

Stewart smiled and nodded his approval, and the girls giggled. That was enough encouragement for another.

"Knock, knock."

"Who's there?"

"Lettuce."

"Lettuce, who?"

"Lettuce in, it's cold out here!"

Stewart laughed and then targeted Louise. "Louise, what do you call a bear with no teeth?"

"I dunno."

"A gummy bear." They all giggled.

He went on. "Knock, knock."

Louise, "Who's there?"

"Wendy."

"Wendy, who?"

"Wendy bell works again, I won't have to knock." They laughed again, and Stewart declared that was a good end to the jokes for the evening.

Soon after cleaning up, Cori announced it was a school night and everyone needed to be in bed on time if they hoped to continue getting together.

"It won't take long. Want to meet for coffee at the Sandwich Club?" Cori was curious to know details about Stewart's rescue mission that were not appropriate for children's ears.

"Definitely."

Stewart left first, and then the girls filed out giggling and talking all at once. Louise asked the inevitable question. "Cori, I thought Micah was your boo. How does Stewart fit in?" Cori let them continue giggling and offered no response. She had no idea what the neighbors thought of the loud display of mirth. But they were all good people.

* * *

Cori arrived at the Sandwich Club to find Stewart waiting with two cups of hot chocolate, and both were still hot.

He looked at her and tipped his head in mild surprise. "You're really good with those girls. That was one of the funniest scenes I've been a part of in a long time, if ever. In a nice way."

She teased back. "Think about the line of work you're in!"

"Makes sense, doesn't it? Anyway, it'll go a long way to replace some images I would like to delete."

"So, you plan to continue?"

"Yeah. Claris and Trent are thinking about working beyond the U.S. borders too, which makes sense. You never know where the evidence is going to take you."

"Why here, in Laurel Ledge?"

"There are a few connections I can't talk about. If you join us . . ."

"In a weak micro-second, I considered it. But I've had my surfeit, thanks."

Cori looked up to see Micah walk into the Sandwich Shop with a small group of people. "Excuse me." She quickly stood up and went over to speak with Micah. Stewart watched closely.

After a few words, she held Micah by the elbow and escorted him to the table where Stewart and she had been sitting together. "I want you two to meet. Micah Flores, this is Stewart Montgomery."

Stewart stood up. "Hey man. Good to meet you."

Micah was less forward, but courteous. "I've heard a lot about you. You're an international hero, I understand."

Stewart replied curtly, "That's up for interpretation, and it's not mine."

As responsive as Stewart was to begin with, Cori noted a mutual frosty atmosphere between them. She decided to do what she encouraged of clients. "Hey, don't make this awkward, you guys. Remember, we're about freedom, not possession." She giggled. Not a little girl giggle, but a sophisticated, light-hearted laugh meant to lighten the mood.

Stewart and Micah both smiled. Micah had a party of folks to return to, so he excused himself. "It was nice seeing both of you. I'll give you a call, Cori." The latter part of the message was quite clever on his part. It wasn't possessive, but it did hint at the closeness that had developed between them. Stewart got the message.

Rather than sitting back down, Stewart said he needed to be on his way. He added, "Cori, I really want you to think about joining the task force. You know it doesn't require being part of the investigations. It's just important to have support for folks as they're about to face a new normality, and before law enforcement does their number on them."

"You make good points. I promise to think about it." Cori was genuinely considering it for the second time.

"Good. It was nice meeting Micah. I'll give you a call, Cori." His tone wasn't mocking, but he was mocking Micah. And he meant it. Cori giggled again. After he left, she proceeded to the table where Micah was seated. She thought he might want to make introductions. With no indication there would be introductions, she simply told them all to have a good night and left.

Chapter 24

Cori mused about the promises of calls from two gentlemen, yet her telephone wasn't ringing. She tried to believe she didn't give a hoot, but she did. Her thoughts vacillated between wondering where she stood with Micah to what Stewart was up to. Micah was an amazing man, and she really wanted to give their relationship a chance. Stewart ran toward danger, and at once she worried about his safety and liked the excitement that surrounded him.

Micah wasn't at the Sunday service at the Landing. Nothing was said of his absence, and several men told of their experiences since recovery had begun for them. Cori invited Della and Reina to her condo for a New England boiled dinner, which had been simmering in the crock pot since just before she retired at midnight the night before.

They helped her set the table with the square china that Della loved. It was fun to see someone excited about such an everyday chore. The discussion was fun, and after clearing, loading the dishwasher, and securing leftovers in the fridge, Della asked Cori if she could make some more valentine cards for the healthcare center visit later that week. Cori told her the materials were in the craft box in the guest room. Della was off on her mission.

Reina watched Della dash off, shook her head and chuckled. "I'm glad we can have a moment to talk without curious ears. I wondered if you had discovered more about your adoption. You may remember telling me about it just before the holidays."

"Yes. I remember the pressure I placed on you about your own story. At the time, I thought our stories might have a common denominator, but I was way off. But no, I haven't found out more. I want to. It's supposed to be a closed matter, so, not only don't I know where to start, I think it's a fool's errand."

"Remember I mentioned that man, Stewart? If I could get his last name, would you want his help? He might have an angle, as they say."

Cori had to stifle her reaction. "Thanks for the suggestion. I need time to think about it if that's okay?"

"Sure. Of course. Ah, I have some good news, Cori."

"Really!" Instantly Cori's interest was piqued. "What is it?"

"Remember Della's dad, the man who was my abusive husband? He died a while back. I didn't mean to imply that's the good news, by the way. Even though he wasn't a very good person. Well, he also was a person of means. Della and I are the closest relatives, and he died without a will. Everything he had is now ours!"

"What!? Reina, you deserve this. Wow. This is so unexpected."

"I know. I can hardly believe it. They asked for birth documents, so I wondered what was going on. They let me know this week. There is some waiting involved, but I will receive a monthly allowance until the funds are released."

"This is great. I'm so happy for you." She gave Reina a bear hug. "What does Della think?"

"I haven't told her. I think I'll play it down when I tell her. Then, as I make changes to our lifestyle, I'll explain why. In fact, if I ask her if there's anything she wants, I know what she'll say. She'll say a dog!"

"Am I prying to ask if you have any plans in particular?"

"Yes. I'm going to study addictions counseling. Even though I would like to help victims, I thought it would make sense to work with people whose lives are out of control first. It might be the best thing I could do for families who might be suffering."

"What a thoughtful plan. Have you applied?"

"Yes. There's a program in Hartford, and I start next week."

"That was fast! How could you do that so soon?"

"It's a short, certificate program. I am applying for a degree to follow up."

"Are you giving up your job?"

"Yes. I'm not very sorry about that." She laughed. "The monthly allowance is much more than we've been living on. I can quit work, buy a more reliable car, go to school and get a bigger apartment."

"Yay, Reina woman!" Cori's demeanor changed. "Does that mean you'll move from Laurel Ledge?"

Reina thought for a minute and then responded. "I'm going to look here first. Della has those wonderful, wacky, friends. I don't want to break them up. I love it here. I do dread the commute though."

"I know you'll work it out. Let me know if I can do anything to help."

"Thank you. You are one of the major reasons I love Laurel Ledge!"

Cori blushed. "Oh, my goodness. What have I done?"

Just at that time, Della bounded back into the room. "Mama, look how many more cards I made!" Cori and Reina looked at the cards. They were nice. Della was a talented crafter and artist.

Reina dropped the news no one really wanted to hear. "We need to get going, Della. I have some things I have to get ready for tomorrow."

"Aww." Della showed her disappointment. She recovered quickly. "Okay. I'm coming back later this week. Bye, Cori. Thanks for dinner!"

"You're welcome. I'll see you later."

* * *

Cori had stayed in touch with Roman, and they were trying to find a new normal given Roman's need to stay close to home and the hospital. Cori knew the possibility of a lung transplant would loom over him for the rest of his life. She didn't know whether he had come to the same realization, but there was no need to emphasize it with him. She no longer dreaded it since it represented his best chance of not being tethered to his home and hospital environments. It was time for a visit, and she decided she would take some R & R with him and Ainsleigh in Arizona after her next long travel assignment. *I must be getting close to being eligible to travel again.*

Her cell rang as she was returning from work on Monday afternoon. It was Claris, so she pulled to the side of the road to talk. "Hey Claris."

"Hi Cori. Can you talk?"

"Yes. How are things?"

Claris sighed deeply. "I am overwhelmed. It's a lot . . . in volume and in its degenerate nature. But anyway, you know that. I wanted to see how things were with you, Roman, and at Amity?"

There wasn't much for news, but Cori thought of a lot to talk about simply because she was talking with Claris. When she stopped for a breather, she asked about Trent.

"He's good. He's feeling much the same as I am. Excited; disgusted. You know."

"Yes, I know."

"I'm also calling to ask if you had given any more thought to helping on the task force. I guess it's not a 'hard sell' the way I've been talking, is it!"

"Not at all!" Cori joked and was serious at the same time. "Stewart made some arguments about my involvement that resonated, but I really don't think it's for me."

"You and Stewart are talking?" Claris didn't hide her surprise and Cori thought she detected some delight as well.

"He came by when Della and her friends were here for dinner and to make valentine cards for the elderly. He even ate with us. We talked at the Sandwich Club over hot chocolate after I delivered the girls home."

"Interesting."

"Micah came in with a group and saw us."

"Oh. Way too interesting."

"They made it a little awkward when I introduced the two of them. I went over to Micah's table after Stewart left, but he didn't deign to introduce me or his friends to me."

"Ouch."

"Oh, the plot thickens. I haven't heard from either since."

"Crimony. Are they children?" Claris was disgusted. "What about the services on Sunday? Did Micah speak with you then?"

"He wasn't there. Nothing was said about him. I did have Reina and Della over for Sunday dinner. Reina had some interesting news."

"Which was . . .?" Claris was pivotal in helping Cori sort out Reina's and Della's involvement in the shelter, Compass Points.

"She will inherit her abuser's wealth. I think it's considerable. It's enough so she has enrolled in college and will quit her job. She intends to buy a car and look for a bigger apartment as well."

"That is such good news, and it is so nice to have good news in this business."

"I know. I will miss them if they don't find something in Laurel Ledge or if she finds the commute to Hartford just won't work well for her." Cori's tone didn't match her words. Overall, she was simply happy for Reina and Della, though she would miss them if they moved. She then remembered Reina's comment about Stewart. "Oh, and Reina recommended that I try to get Stewart to help me find out about my biological parents."

Claris chuckled. "Life is full of paradoxes. Did you tell her how well you know him?"

"No. I feel like a liar at this point. I'm so far into it, I have no idea how to unravel the story for her."

"You need to do it. You'll think of a way. She sounds like a sweet but very wise woman. I don't think there is much that would shock her or shake her faith in you."

"Yeah. I will face it and soon."

"Will you hire Stewart?"

"No. He doesn't even know I'm adopted!"

"Is there a reason why not?"

"No. There isn't. Not anymore. I think we're friends. Have you heard from him?"

"He's here training, too. He's in a very different cluster from us right now. I think we'll all come together by the end of the week and be back in town by next week. At least for a while."

"Oh. Good. Maybe I'll hear from him then."

"Call him!" Claris was more encouraging than chiding.

"Yeah. I could. I probably will." Cori spoke as she was thinking it through.

"Call Micah, too." Claris was a little pushier this time.

"I will. It makes sense. Thanks Claris. It's great talking with you."

"Bye."

"Bye."

* * *

Cori decided Claris was right. She was going to take the high road and made the calls. She was having trouble deciding whom she would call first.

"Micah Flores."

"Hi! It's Cori."

"Oh, Cori. Sorry. I didn't even look at the call ID. How are you?"

"I'm good. I missed you at the Landing today. For the last few days, in fact."

Silence, or was it a pause. Cori waited to be sure.

"I didn't tell you I was traveling the latter part of the week and over the weekend."

"No." She was providing information he already knew. "I feel there was an intent?"

"Maybe." He answered as if he wasn't sure.

"Are you hurt because of Stewart?"

"Maybe."

"Does it make any difference that I've told you all there is to know about that evening?"

"I don't think you told me why he just drops by your apartment. . . something I haven't had the nerve to do yet."

"And, you are a different person from Stewart . . . not that I wasn't surprised to see him!" Cori was convinced she was being transparent in her feelings.

"Has he explained himself?"

"I haven't heard from him."

"I hate that you were over there together and now have this history together."

"And this didn't help."

"No, it hurt. It confirmed that there was something to it."

"Something, how?"

"You don't know . . . I don't know. . . I have a feeling he knows."

Cori was taken aback. *Stewart had said so. Why wouldn't Micah feel slighted.* Suddenly she felt as if she had been coy about this. In retrospect, she was in denial about Micah being justified in how he felt.

She made a stab at being truly genuine this time. "He hasn't made any moves, Micah. Obliquely he *has* expressed interest, but he is respecting the relationship you and I have. And, honestly, he has won me over as a friend."

"Uh huh."

"Where do you and I go from here?"

"He hasn't called?"

"No."

"Are you going to call him?"

"I was thinking about it. He is with Claris and Trent in training, but they only have seen glimpses of him. But, if you object, our relationship takes precedence."

"I'm not going to tell you not to call him, Cori."

"You wish I didn't want to."

"Yeah. I guess that's accurate."

"It's so strange. I wouldn't have considered it a week ago."

"That's why showing up at your doorstep is so significant. I think he's a player who knows what he is doing."

"Maybe that's part of it. I'm telling myself a future call is as much about asking him for help about my adoption."

"Do you think that's a good idea?" Micah was sounding more intense and less hurt.

"I don't know. I don't expect to be able to do anything on my own." Cori emphasized the last few words.

"There are *other* private investigators." Micah was tongue-in-cheek.

"Yes. There are. Let's forget it for now. Call me when you return? You didn't tell me where you are."

"I hope folks will get used to my absences and the fact that they're not announced at services or printed in the bulletin.

Sometimes it's confidential and sometimes not. And, to answer your specific question, this is one of those times I can't share with you, either. I'm sorry. But I could have told you I would be away."

"I hope we're okay."

"Let's take it a day at a time, once again."

"Okay by me. Goodnight." She tried to sound glib, but she was confused. "Oh wait! I have some good news." She excitedly told him Reina's news. His response startled her a bit.

"Oh. It sounds good. I hope it works out that way. Goodnight."

Chapter 25

Della and her friends exited the school bus at Cori's condo complex, and they were all talking excitedly. They could hardly get down the bus steps. One would turn around and hold the others up while she talked to someone behind her, and then someone would be beside someone so that they couldn't proceed down the steps . . . it was mini-pandemonium!

Eventually they were all in the parking lot and spied Cori waiting for them. They ran to her, each trying to tell her something very important, once again, all at once. Cori laughed and tried to get a handle on what they were willing to do next. "Okay, okay. I'm excited too. Shall we go upstairs, get our cards and snacks and get in the car?"

"Yeah!" It was in unison as a cheer.

Cori loved their chatter and enthusiasm but thought it was fitting to have a word with them before entering to see the

residents. "So, you know whom we're going to visit, right?"
"Yup."

"You know that older people are very sensitive to noise, and they can get confused."

"Really?"

"Yes. What do you think we should do?"

"We should be quiet."

"I agree. We'll walk in and not say anything. We'll wait for directions, but here is how I think it will go. We'll help the activities director wheel residents to the living room. Then we'll hand out some of the song sheets to those who want them. We'll sing some of the old love songs. We'll collect the song sheets from those who want to give them back. Many of them will want to keep them. Let's let them, okay?"

"Yeah."

"Then we'll have the cookies. Who do you think should get the cookies first?"

"People who live here."

"Right."

"Then we'll give them the valentines. Sound like a plan?"

"Let's light this candle!" Louise was a stitch.

When the group was finished and assembled outside, Louise declared, "We hit that one out of the park! I was scared to go in there to begin with."

Cori knew they were a good group, but she never envisioned they would do so well. She agreed with Louise. "I can't thank you enough, girls. It means so much for the residents to see young people. Some of them don't have families or their families are so busy they don't get to see them often. This was very special."

Louise continued with questions. "How did you meet your friend, Phyllis?"

"She was a good friend of my mom's. Sort of a mentor to her. I continued to visit her after my mom died."

"What about the sign language?"

Cori chuckled. "Oh, that. We have our own sign language. The one you saw was to handle repetition, which is common for older folks. After repeating something for the fifth time in one conversation, I hold up six digits as a sign that she's said the same thing over and over."

Louise chuckled this time. "But Cori, Phyllis was signaling to you!"

Once again, Cori had no response.

* * *

On her solo trip home, Cori decided to drop by the Landing. She found Micah in his office. "Hi. Is everything okay?" Micah seemed caught off guard but was quick with his question.

"Yes, everything is fine. I just came back from an afternoon with my young friends, and I thought I would see if you are in. I missed you."

He came from around the desk. Despite his unsettled feelings about their relationship, he was enticed by her presence. He went over to her and slowly took her in his arms. He sniffed her hair as he gently brushed his lips through the beautiful strands. He began to kiss her lightly on the ear, the cheek, and then on the mouth. Then, hard on the mouth. Not for the first time, his open mouth ravished hers.

Suddenly he became aware of his surroundings. It wasn't Micah's practice to use his office in this way. "Can I see you tonight?"

"Yes."

"I have some things to finish up here, including a resident I promised to visit before leaving."

"That's fine. Just come by my condo when you're finished."

"That sounds great, but I don't think I should. I'll text you the plans."

Cori picked up some groceries on her way home. She was headed for the bedroom to change into something special to wear for dinner when she received a text from Micah. "Meet me at the Rolling Hills Tree Farm on Route 11. Warm layers; appetite."

What a nice idea. A sleigh ride.

The tree farm provided "cut your own trees" during the Christmas season as well as sleigh rides all winter through the massive wooded hills. There was a mountain top café at one of the summits called Lone Pine Lodge.

Cori donned her silk long underwear for a first layer, a layer of winter leggings, a cable knit sweater, and a down jacket. A cable knit cap, mittens, and infinity scarf finished off her ensemble. She received the latter from Ainsleigh and Roman for Christmas, and she was quite sure they didn't find them at a brick and mortar store in Phoenix. More likely when they were able to sneak a purchase without her seeing while they shopped at L.L. Bean over the Thanksgiving holiday.

Under normal circumstances, she would wear a face muffler for the sleigh ride. But that wouldn't be part of the outwear when out when Micah. It turned out to be a good choice. It was understood that Micah would not be progressing their physical relationship beyond caresses and kissing. Spiritually, physically, and vocationally, it was the only decision for him. He and Cori both knew that the culture in which they lived would dictate he was perhaps the only man alive with those convictions, and he knew that attitude led to the practice becoming less and less a fabric of the society. He had had many relationships, and he understood the intimacy is often vapid when one rushes to the physical as a priority over a true emotional commitment. Finding a partner with the same convictions was a priority.

That said, the sleigh ride was a wonderful venue for passionate kissing. Micah had reserved a sleigh for two and a driver, and the trip to the café was one long buss. It took them a moment to separate and exit the sleigh after arriving. They may have been hungry at one time, but it no longer seemed important.

Dine they did, though. They found butternut squash ravioli on the menu, which they both loved. It was sautéed in sage-infused butter mixed with a cream sauce with a hint of balsamic and maple syrup. Their appetites were revived with New England clam chowder and followed by the ravioli.

Their conversation was lively and focused on continuing to get to know each other's story. Micah still had many questions. "How did you decide to become a counselor? It seems with the medical involvement you might have chosen one of the many professions that would build on the knowledge you gained with Roman's illness."

"I was never inured to medical knowledge. I did only what I had to do. It could have been because of spending so much time in hospitals. Mom didn't work outside of the home for much of my life, but she did have a degree in psychology and worked as a victim advocate in the district attorney's office for a couple of years just before adopting Roman. I was young, but I had a vague idea of what it meant to be a counselor, and I was fascinated. No matter what I dabbled in for courses in college, my interest was always in the psychology section of the course catalog. So, I just went with it."

She turned the conversation to Micah. "You know so much about my brother, what about you? Do you have siblings?"

"It's a fairly big family. I have two brothers and a sister. My sister is married, and I have a niece and nephew. They're the best kids, even if I'm a little partial. They live in San Diego, so I don't get to see them very often. It will be less often now, I suppose. Her husband is a software developer. They do well.

One of my brothers is a major in the army. He isn't married, at least yet. He doesn't mind moving, so he's all over the place. Right now, he's near my sister, but I don't think he's as wild about the kids as I am."

"Are you wild about kids in general?" Cori thought it was as good a time as any to ask.

"Are you asking if I want kids, eventually?" He had a slightly playful tone.

"Do you?"

"I think so. But I want to let it play out. It depends on with whom, and their wishes, and where we are in life when the time is right. If enough time passes, I think I'll pass on the job. I'm closing in on it." Micah had almost a decade on Cori regarding age.

Cori was encouraging, "Older parents are fine. My parents were on the older side. Maybe that's why I always felt as though I was born old, though. Many of their likes, customs, and just culture in general was so out of date compared to the parents of my friends. And I did lose them when Roman and I were young. I really needed them. But, that was an accident and not because of their age."

"Oh, I didn't intend to be critical of couples who become parents late in life. I know it's not for me."

"I understand. But I think we left out a brother."

"Oh. I suppose in the lexicon of counselors, that would be a parapraxis!" His voice was a bit sheepish.

"You aren't the best of friends?" Cori tried to be gentle in her curiosity.

"Well, we were. Something happened to change that."

"Are you okay talking about it?" She really wanted to know, but she wasn't sure how hard to push.

"Yeah. I'll tell you about it. He had a job like the one I have now. He was in Wisconsin at the time. Married, but no children. The rescue mission he ran was supported by area churches and individuals. A ton of volunteer time was typical from residents in the area.

"Well, he started drinking heavily. He continued even after it was strongly suspected. I tried to talk some sense into him at his wife's request. I went a little overboard in trying, I guess. When he assured me that he could handle it on his own, and then did nothing, I lost my temper and promptly told the Executive Board and insisted that he resign. He finally agreed to detox.

"Initially he did resign, but someone on the board decided they wanted the mission involved in his rehabilitation. So, they held his resignation in abeyance and got him counseling. Long story short, he was returned to his job in a few weeks."

"How do you feel about that?"

"It's a wrong-headed decision, no matter how you look at it. Without getting into the details, big picture is the churches were split in whether to support the decision. Half of them dropped their support, and they should have. Volunteers were split on the decision, and it had a polarizing effect on staff as well. The supporters seemed puffed up in their loving and forgiving spirits. The detractors were criticized as judgmental and cruel."

"What do you think should have happened?" Cori's curiosity was even more intense.

"He should have really manned-up and followed through with the resignation." Micah was adamant.

"Would he be able to find another job like that?"

"That's the point. If he was sullied for another organization, why in heck wasn't he sullied for the organization he betrayed so flagrantly! He had been preaching, leading devotionals and therapy groups, speaking at churches, and so many other roles where he bamboozled those he was supposedly serving as an example."

"What role does forgiveness play?"

"The drinking? Forgiven. The failure to resign? That's tougher. He has never asked for forgiveness. He blatantly continued regardless of the fallout. Eventually he left the job, but it was after the damage had been done. His wife also passed away a year ago. Cancer."

"Oh."

"A mess. Yes."

"Do you two speak?"

"Well, yes. I don't confide in him or seek him out in the way I used to. But we talk. I try to keep up with what he's doing. He's a social worker in Portland, Oregon. Just my point. There are other jobs out there."

"How did the rest of your family deal with it?"

"They're a little more understanding of him than I am. They didn't know of the deceit and lies involved in trying to hold onto his job. They thought he should have resigned, but it didn't roil with them as it did with me."

"Did it change your relationship with your other brother and sister?"

"Some. I confess I just don't feel on the same page with them. Tres convinced them I came on too strong with him, and I did. To my face, he credited me with saving him from hitting rock bottom. I wish I could have a sense of humor about the folks who refuse to be judgmental of him but are very judgmental of the way I handled things."

"Family stuff. Sometimes it just has to play out over time. Just like it does with close friends." She wondered if he would get the point.

"I get your point. I only wanted to encourage you to speak with your friend again." He seemed sheepish, and she regretted the oblique criticism when he was so vulnerable.

The conversation returned to a normal banter gradually while they enjoyed a shared dessert of double chocolate cheesecake. They left half of it.

The return sleigh ride was not as passionate, but they cuddled and chatted the whole way. They kissed goodnight in the parking lot. He apologized if his family's story ruined the evening, and she assured him it didn't. "Call me." Those were her parting words as he opened her car door and watched her until she drove out of the lot.

Chapter 26

Cori hadn't heard from Stewart, but she decided against seeking him out. She was afraid of hurting Micah.

She was on a break between counseling sessions when Stewart walked into her office. Her door was open, and he startled her a bit when he spoke. "Hey fellow prisoner. What's up?"

"Stewart! When did you get back?"

"Last night. I think you'll be seeing Claris too."

"Good. How did it go?"

"It's good. There's so much to learn. I'm not much for book-learnin'. Give me the practical. But, the statistics and patterns of movement are something we have to keep up with."

"Where to from here?"

"I have a private job in the area. I don't think it will take long."

"You can't tell me about it, of course."

"Of course." He smirked. "How about some lunch?" He gave her an askance look.

She hesitated.

"Is there a problem? I'm a problem for Micah, right?" He was being honest but not accusatory.

"Sort of. He is really uneasy about our relationship."

"*Our* as in you and me or *our* as in you and him?"

"Mostly you and me."

"He should be, actually. I thought of staying away. I tried. It's been awhile. I don't know if you noticed."

Cori didn't answer.

"But, I want to be friends. I won't move in. Promise. I don't suppose I can convince him of that, can I?"

"Probably not."

"What about a snack in your café here in the building?"

"I would still have to tell him about it."

"Let's ask Claris, too. That's what friends do."

"We can try!"

Claris was able to join them, which was the perfect solution as far as Cori was concerned. They chatted for a long time about their work in LA. Claris and Trent were going back soon, and essentially it represented a temporary relocation. Since Stewart had worked as an extractor for some time already, his home base would remain the same and his work would take him wherever. He would have to meet regularly in LA with the rest of the team.

Seemingly out of the blue, Cori asked Stewart if he still worked for Compass Points now that he wasn't affiliated with Lourdes. Claris seemed uncomfortable, and Stewart was curious as to what was her point.

"I have to keep my clients confidential. You know that."

"It's personal. Claris knows this, but I never told you I'm adopted."

"Oh. You're right. I didn't know that. Is that why you're curious about Compass Points? Is there a connection?"

"I don't know. Remember our conversation about my friends Reina and Della?"

"Yup. I'm not going to forget that!" He feigned a frightened look.

"When I found out the truth about Reina, I started suspecting that I'm related to either Dr. Dallas, or Lourdes. Or both. Who knows?"

"Wo. Wait. What a leap! Where'd that come from?" Stewart typically wasn't surprised, but if anyone could floor him, it was Cori.

"It's just some hunches I put together. My adoption is as closed as they get. So, I have no idea. We only found out about it by investigating Roman's adoption. We found a random piece of paper that should have been destroyed."

"But you want to know."

"Yes." She wondered why he wasn't volunteering. Something was up, but she didn't know what it was. "Reina suggested I have you look into it."

"I can't right now. Here's a suggestion. Start by having your ancestry done."

Cori was intrigued. *Why hadn't I thought of that?* "That's a great idea. Why didn't I think of that?"

"It's what I do."

Chapter 27

Conversations between Cori and Micah were by text and phone for a few days. A travel opportunity with a colleague came up for him that involved fundraising. Cori informed him of her lunch with Stewart and Claris. She wasn't sure how to broach the subject of Stewart's promise not to "move in" on her for a relationship beyond friendship, but she blundered through. She couldn't gauge Micah's reaction. She gave herself credit for trying.

Micah thought DNA testing was a realistic step for Cori to pursue. He couldn't help resenting Stewart's involvement and wished he had thought of the idea.

* * *

Cori returned to her condo to find the test results from her DNA testing several weeks later. She tore open the results.

There were so many statistical analyses and a map. She had looked at images of results online when she became interested in getting her own results. Many have various regions circled on a map and a percentage of each of the regions represented on an individual's DNA results. Hers were stark in the lack of diversity. The Baltic states were circled. Eastern Europe 100%. This was shocking. She fully expected Western Europe. She needed to talk to someone about what this meant. *Well, I know what this means. I need help processing the information.*

Her second thought was whether this eliminated Lourdes. With a given name like Lourdes, and a surname like Dumont, which was her family name, she had concluded that Lourdes had a good deal of Western Europe in her DNA. But who really knows about these things.

She decided to rule out her suspicions in a very bold move. She wished she had done this before. Dr. Dallas typically volunteered at Compass Points evenings, so she was going to drop by and take a chance that evening.

Cori was met by a receptionist when she walked into the small, humble reception area of Compass Points. The receptionist was pregnant, so Cori deduced that she was also a resident. Cori told her she needed to see Dr. Dallas and that she was a potential donor.

"Why don't you come back during the day when a full-time staff member is on duty and will be equipped to consult on the options for benefactors?" The receptionist asked a question, but it was an oblique way of putting up a barrier.

Cori insisted. "I have some apprehensions about Compass Points that only Dr. Dallas can answer."

All of Cori's statements were true so far. The receptionist asked her to take a seat and disappeared. She reappeared with Dr. Dallas, whom Cori recognized from a previous encounter at the hospital when Byron's baby girl was born.

He asked her into a small office down the hall and left the door open. He was genial but not overly friendly. She gave him a lot of credit. He could have been openly annoyed.

"What can I do for you?"

"I apologize for the intrusion, because that's what this is. Though I do intend to leave a contribution, and I do have some apprehensions about Compass Points, despite the good work that happens here."

He looked stoic and barely tolerant of what she had to say. "Go ahead."

"I know this is blunt and insulting, but I'm adopted, and I've been blocked from finding out about my adoption. I believe everyone deserves to know about their heritage."

"I can understand."

"I think you are my dad, or your wife is my mom, or perhaps both."

He looked as though he had been punched in the stomach. He turned from her and faced the window, though the blinds were closed. He seemed deep in thought. Without looking back, he finally broke the silence. "What caused that conclusion?"

She told him. She recounted the ostracism from her best friend, what she saw as Lourdes' possible involvement through the promise of a dream job for said best friend, and how the job had materialized. She summarized what Lourdes had against her. First her involvement with Reina and Della, and her confirmation that Lourdes was instrumental in having them relocated, even though Cori later found out there was no reason for Lourdes to be threatened by their presence. She concluded with the story of finding out about her adoption, the involvement of Lourdes' law firm, and her new suspicion that the target on her back went beyond what Lourdes suspected of Dr. Dallas's involvement with Reina but rather the direct involvement of the Dallases with her birth.

He looked at her for a short time before speaking. "You mentioned Stewart."

"Yes, I know Stewart well. We were hostages recently while we tried to save an American consultant from a ring of human traffickers in China. We ended up in Kazakhstan."

"I didn't realize." He then went back to her inquiry. "Who were your adoptive parents?"

"She told him about the Sellers."

"What's your birthday?"

"She told him . . . at least what she thought it was. She threw in the part about her DNA testing."

"Neither of us is your parent, Cori. I knew that before you told me about the DNA testing. However, you might be right about being involved in your birth."

"What?"

"I can only explain by providing a lot of confidential information."

"I'm a counselor. Let's consider it therapy. I will only divulge it if there is a danger to yourself or others."

He laughed. "Okay. Listen. I am aware of my reputation with some folks. Luckily, the ones who need to know the truth realize it's perpetrated by my lovely, fiery, accomplished wife. She is confident in every way, except when it comes to my work. She has never adjusted to the way I work with women.

"Many of the stories of women who come to Compass Points are sketchy, so her suspicions over the years have centered on stories she fabricates about me and some of the women here. I knew about Stewart. Eventually I figured out I was being surveilled by Lourdes."

"Does Stewart know you have his number?"

"I suppose, but we never talk about it."

"What does this do to your marriage?"

"I adore Lourdes. She rules the roost in our marriage. Compass Points and my practice are off-limits to her. I don't tell her about them. I try to convince her at various intervals that I am not involved with patients or anyone, but I don't give supporting evidence."

Cori couldn't adapt to this information. Her assumptions were difficult to overcome. She shook her head slightly, but quickly, as if confused. She was confused. She did remember one comment and came back to it. "How, then, might you have been involved in my birth?"

"On occasion, we work with women who have been the victims of trafficking or being held against their will. This started years and years ago, before public awareness was raised. Some of the women have been helped by extraction. Others have escaped and found us. I think your mother may have been someone who escaped and found us."

"Do you know that for sure?"

"I don't remember everyone who comes through. Trafficking from Eastern Europe is very common since the mid-nineties. It wasn't prior to the break-up of the Soviet Union given travel restrictions and state-control over everything, including crime. Since your total heritage was Eastern Europe, I suspect that your biological mother's captor was your biological father rather than some random john in New York City. He probably took a shine to her and 'kept' her for himself against her will. The secrecy of the adoption could have been as much for your protection as hers. I have referred a few over the years to my wife's firm, which probably feeds her suspicions. But they are the best.

"As I talk about it, it sounds familiar. I promise to go over our files around the time of your birth and see what I find out. The chances are, I won't be able to divulge any information I find. Please brace yourself. Do you mind if I use your name and ask Lourdes for legal advice?"

"You're serious?" Cori was incredulous. Then she thought about it for a moment. "That's incredible. It would solve more than a few problems, wouldn't it?"

"It would."

"Thank you." Stunned, Cori walked out of the office and the building in a daze. As she thought about the encounter with Dr. Dallas, she wondered if he knew who she was and that's why he let her in. She trusted very few people.

Chapter 28

Days went by without any word from Dr. Dallas. Cori, Della, and the girls took in a movie matinee on a Saturday afternoon for a change of pace. Louise wanted to know when they would plan their next community service project. This girl never ceased to tickle Cori. She gathered idioms, jokes, and phrases like a stick in cotton candy.

Della had been routinely inviting her friends to services at the Landing, but none had accepted. That all changed. Two of them asked Cori for a ride. Louise said her mom was coming too.

It was a bit lively in the row of chairs with Reina and Cori the next morning at the Landing. She loved their excitement but hoped they could be settled a bit for when the service commenced. She warned Micah ahead of time.

There was no reason to doubt the girls. They had risen to every occasion so far, and they did on Sunday. They all wanted to go to the Sandwich Club following the service. Reina piped up, "Good idea. My treat."

Both Cori and Louise's mom said they would help, but they didn't argue the point then. Della suggested they wait for Micah and ask him to join them. Cori looked around at the eight females and couldn't anticipate how he would respond. But she wasn't about to answer for him.

She left it up to Della to ask. When he came to greet them, Della barely waited for the introductions to be accomplished. "Mr. Flores, we're all going to the Sandwich Club. Mama's treat. We want you to come!"

He bent over a bit, raised his eyebrows and said, "You do?"

The lyrical group of friends, in *unison*, exclaimed, "Yes! Please!"

"I'd love to then."

Cori had permission to drive the girls who were Della's guests, so Micah went with them in her car. The Sandwich Club was the gathering place for adults, but it was a special treat for the kids to dine there. The excitement resumed in a big way outside the restaurant as they approached the entrance. Cori envisioned a noisy, embarrassing entrance if they persisted. As delightful as it was, it would be a startling occurrence to those dining inside.

"Girls! Girls!"

In unison. "What?"

"Remember the chat before we went to sing to the residents at the healthcare center a couple of weeks ago?"

"Uh huh!" Shrieked in unison. "We need to get a grip!" Spoken by lingo Louise.

"Okay. Good. You understand what we need to do, right?"

"Yup." And just like that, they pranced into the restaurant with manners that could make Emily Post proud. Cori certainly was.

The girls were amazing. They ordered two sandwiches to cut and share and a large order of fries. They decided to sit at a table of their own, and they did their best to eat all the food even while chattering the whole time.

Micah, Reina, Cori, and Lottie, Louise's mom, had an awkward beginning to their conversation. Lottie broke the silence. "I appreciated what you said this morning, Mr. Flores."

"Please call me Micah."

"Okay. I used to attend church with my parents, but I got busy and let it slip as a priority. I would like to talk to you some time about the verses you read from Romans. I liked that. The 'Roman Road'."

"Let's set up a time." Micah accessed the calendar on his phone, and he and Lottie chatted as they organized the exit of this lively group.

In addition to paying the bill, Reina offered to drive the girl guests home. Micah had to return to the Landing for his car and to tie up some loose ends. He and Cori decided to get some tea in the café of the Landing. A couple of residents having some dessert and coffee were nearby, and Micah greeted them as did Cori.

Cori warmed her hands on her cup and poised herself to tell Micah something difficult for her to say. "Micah, I don't think I told you I went to see Dr. Dallas."

He tried not to look startled, but he was blown away. "I don't think you did. When was this?"

"Sometime last week, I think."

"Where?" He wasn't going to stop with the questions.

"His office at Compass Points."

"Did you make an appointment or what?"

"Just barged in. I almost think he knows who I am."

"How?"

"I don't know. The hostage situation. The distant past. I think he knows more than he is telling me."

"Do you still think he might be your father, then?"

"No. I did the DNA testing, and it was totally the Baltic countries. I was startled, and it prompted me to settle the question of him and Lourdes. The results made me doubt it was them, but I couldn't rule it out. What did I know about their respective DNA's? So, I asked."

"I don't know where to continue with questions. Maybe just the end of the story, and then we'll back up?"

"I think when I told him about the DNA results and my birthdate, he remembered the story. He's going to look at records, but he might not be able to tell me anything due to confidentiality. He's going to check with a lawyer." She looked at him to see if he would pick up on the lawyer part. She already had told him too much given she had promised confidentiality, but she wasn't going to talk about the Dallas's marriage. "Remember, this has to be confidential. I'm telling you as my Pastor."

He chuckled. "Nice rationalization. Is the lawyer going to be his wife, perchance?"

"Why don't we just say a lawyer, okay?"

"Fine. Have you heard anything?"

"Not a word."

"What next then?" He dreaded the answer but thought he should ask in case he could head her off from another rash move.

"I'll wait a bit longer." She sounded convincing.

"Then what?" He wanted to know whether she had a plan.

"I don't know. I guess I'll cross that bridge when I think I've waited long enough."

He proceeded cautiously. "May I comment on all of this? It's kind of 'judgy'."

"Tread lightly."

He sighed, deeply. "I'll try. Are you willing to consider your successes? You found out the truth about Dr. Dallas and Lourdes, *and* it sounds like his wife will know the truth about you as well, if that ever was an issue. I wouldn't have the guts to do what you did. Well done. But, given the parties involved pledged that the details of your adoption would remain secret, is it possible that it's best to leave it that way?"

"Ah, ouch! That feels like a heel stomp!"

"So much for treading lightly?"

"Yeah!"

"At least you have a sense of humor about it."

"I don't. Sometimes it takes me a minute to lose my temper."

"Oh. Are you going to lose your temper?"

"No. I think you had to say it. If you didn't, someone would."

"Then, would you consider it?"

"Not for a minute."

"Okay."

"Okay."

"Well, I hope it works out. Really."

"Thanks."

"Are you still mad?"

"No. People just don't get it. I guess I wished that you would."

"I'll try."

"I hope so. If I had to guess, I'll bet you'll try to stop me whenever I hit a wall."

"I just don't want you to get hurt."

"Micah, I do hurt. This will be a constant hurt. Yes, I may not succeed. Yes, I may find rejection even with answers. It isn't about preventing hurt. It's about finding out."

"Okay. Sorry."

"Don't apologize for your opinion. I wish you were willing to not put obstacles in my way. That is what would add to the hurt. That is what would make me wish I had said nothing to you."

"I'll try."

"I'm going to get going."

"Okay. I hope I didn't ruin a wonderful day. I had a good time with your friends, grown and half-grown."

"Yeah. I'm glad. It was fun. Bye." She kissed him on the lips and thought about how much she loved the taste of his kisses. It helped.

Chapter 29

One would never know how often I think of contacting Jessalyn given how long it's been since I have done anything about the good intentions. I can at least text.

"Hey Jessalyn. Just missing you. I think of you often."

The condo was a dust bin, so she took the cordless off the wall and gave the floors a once over. It was so bad she even put on the dust attachment and dusted furniture and baseboards. She felt appropriately self-righteous. The feeling would last for weeks until she realized she was again living in a dust bin. She was putting the stick back on the charger when her cell rang with Jessalyn's ringtone.

"Hi!" Cori was pleased.

"Hey. Thanks for texting. I wanted to chat. When is a good time?"

"Anytime. What are you doing now?"

"Not much. I have a husband who just left on a business trip, and the kids are off with friends as always."

"How about coming over and we'll make some of my killer cheese fondue."

"Uh, do you have any chocolate?"

"Yup. Pick up some strawberries and pound cake."

"Will do."

Cori had the cheese fondue all prepared when Jessalyn arrived. They cut the French bread and enjoyed their entrée. Cori had the chocolate prepared in a double boiler on the stove, but she turned off the heat when they decided to take a break from eating.

They brought their hot chocolate to the living room, and Cori inquired about Jessalyn's family. Jessalyn's son and daughter were busy with cello and flute, and both loved to attend high school basketball games. To say they were busy was an understatement. Cori hardly saw them anymore.

"My husband and I are 'like ships that pass in the night.' I know that's trite, but I didn't believe it until now. With the kids independent, he took on a management role at the insurance company. He won't say he regrets it, but, well, let's just say at least my long shifts come to an end. He must simply walk away to get some sleep. I'm looking forward to our vacation. Did I tell you we're going to Paris in April?"

"No. Good. When did that come up?"

"One of those random flyers was faxed to my department a few weeks ago. We thought it was a good deal. We need it."

"Kids?"

"Nope. Grandma is coming just to be an anchor. That's what we're saying. But I want an update on you."

"Oh. Well. Where did we leave off?"

"I told you to call Micah and Stewart."

"You did not. That was Claris. I told you about it."

Jessalyn chuckled. "I know. Good memory. So?"

"I have to think about it. I don't remember whether Micah called me, or I called him, but we did resume our relationship. I'd say we're together. I didn't call Stewart, but he appeared at my door when I was making a light supper with Della, Louise, Janney, and Sarah. He was great with the kids. He and I met for dessert at the Sandwich Club after I dropped the girls off at home. Guess who walked in?"

"Who? Wait. No. Micah?"

"Yup."

"Ouch!"

"Yup."

"What happened?"

"Cold shoulder, worked it through. The only time I've spoken with Stewart since is at Amity's café along with Claris. He promised not to move in on Micah. I assured Micah we were just friends. I don't think that's going to be possible. Micah bristles even if Stewart's name is mentioned."

"What do you think about it?"

"I understand, but I also hate it."

"Did you want to stay friends."

"I would prefer that. But Micah's resentment is too high a price."

"Yeah. I guess. Do you think it's serious with Micah?"

"It could become serious. Sure."

"Are you thinking he's your soulmate?"

Cori was silent, thinking. Jessalyn spoke again to break the silence. "I'll take that as a 'not yet' at best and a 'no' as a definite possibility."

"It's just little things that make me wonder . . . on occasion. We're attracted to each other, but I know he doesn't 'get me.' But maybe the bar's too high when it comes to understanding me."

"I get the feeling Stewart does."

Cori felt like she had been punched. "I want to be mad that you said that, but he does. But does that mean anything? He's so 'out there' himself. Not too much shocks him, including me."

"I think it's more than that. Maybe you should consider there's a real connection between you."

On most days, Cori tried to avoid thinking about it. *What's the point? Stewart's lifestyle is radical. How could he consider a serious relationship? I can't tell anyone about it, either. And, he a libertarian!* She smiled a bit at the last thought.

Jessalyn looked at her quizzically. "So?"

"Micah and I will work it out. Maybe the differences we have are small."

"Do you have plans for Valentine's Day, for instance?"

"Yes. Everything is a surprise, though. How about you?"

"I took a page out of Micah's playbook, and I'm taking Tom on a sleigh ride and dinner."

"Oh. You'll love it. Try not to pry about anything controversial at the end of the evening, though."

"Okay. And, how is Roman?" Jessalyn and Cori were close. Jessalyn didn't mind prodding, but she had no intention of making Cori uncomfortable.

"The same. He's still on the transplant list, and I'm not flipping out about it. It might be for the best. But right now, he's holding his own. He's getting out of the house and having a life that is nearer normality. Not like before this latest bout, but a relief compared to being housebound. Ainsleigh recovered from the flu."

"Good to hear."

Cori changed the subject. "I think I'm ready for dessert. How about you?"

"Yeah."

While they were dipping their fruit and cake in the velvety mixture, Cori broached the subject of her visit to Dr. Dallas. She didn't want to breech confidentiality, so she kept her comments to things she had discussed with Jessalyn before her visit.

"Jessalyn, the rumors about Dr. Dallas aren't true. I promised to keep our discussion confidential, but there's a good explanation for the rumors and why he doesn't do anything to stop them. He might be an okay guy. And you know I can be tough on people."

"I wish you could say more, but I will take your word for it. So, do you know any more about your biological parents beyond the DNA testing?" "No. I'm not out of hope, yet, and Dr. Dallas might be able to find more information. But even if he does, chances are he won't be able to tell me about it."

"Bummer. Too bad you can't get Stewart to help."

"You're not the first to suggest it. Oh! Speaking of Reina, who was the other one who suggested it, she has inherited quite a bit of money from her abuser's estate!"

"Cool. I love good news!"

They had their surfeit of chocolate for the evening, and Jessalyn brought the evening to a close.

Cori mindlessly binge-watched episodes of *The Office* before retiring.

Chapter 30

A typical valentine's celebration for Cori involved showing those around her how much she appreciated them. It was about Yankee Candles, chocolates, or flowers purchased for co-workers, homemade cards for healthcare center residents, and dinner with family and friends. This was the first time in a long time that she was celebrating true romance.

It was romantic. Micah's sleigh ride was spontaneous and perfect, and she had no expectation that he could top that on Valentine's Day or any other day. Travel for work had kept them from getting together for well over a week, but they texted and spoke on the telephone often. He apologized soon after that Sunday afternoon coffee at the Landing and at the same time asked if they could spend the evening of Valentine's Day together.

She was told to dress warm, but she didn't suspect another sleigh ride. She was later arriving home than she wanted to be due to some last-minute mini-emergencies at work. She had no time for lunch, so she was looking forward to a delicious meal. Some thought had been given to her outfit, and she decided to wear a dress, which was black but not too little since she wanted to wear leggings for warmth. She packed everything in one of her huge handbags to include some additional layers if needed.

Micah picked her up at 4:00 in the afternoon. For the first time, he was in her apartment. He kissed her hello, and the greeting continued for a long time. They hadn't seen each other in too long. When he released her, his voice was raspy as he said, "We have reservations. We need to get going. I hope there will be more of that later."

Cori couldn't tell where they were headed, and eventually they drove into what she knew was a small airport parking lot. He exited the car and hurried over to open her door. "Are you ready?"

"For anything, I guess."

They headed toward a helipad with a chopper and a pilot waiting for them. Cori looked at Micah. "Really? Where are we going?"

He teased. "Do you think I'm going to answer that?"

They got in the helicopter and off it flew. She now understood the reason for the early hour. She knew enough about the terrain to realize they were headed for New York City, at least that was her best guess. They held hands as the copter pilot pointed out landmarks. He changed course and took them north along the Hudson River and the Catskill mountains.

"This is amazing, Micah."

"I've been wanting to do this since I moved East. I wanted you with me more than anything."

"Thank you."

Before darkness set in, they arrived at another helipad in Brooklyn, where an Uber was waiting to take them to Bleeker Street for pizza. It was a modest, early dinner, but just as good as the celebrity reviews claimed. Micah had other plans for the evening as well.

They strolled over to Washington Square Park, sat on a bench, and took in the sights. Cori loved the arch and the people were always a study. They couldn't resist some heavy necking. Micah gently pulled away and said, we have one more thing to do.

Cori didn't know how he arranged Uber transportation on such a busy evening. She didn't allow herself to think about the cost. The Uber wove in and out of traffic that resembled a parking lot. She was an amazing, scary driver. They arrived on Forty-Second Street in about a half hour, but sat on the street unable to move for several minutes before Micah suggested that they could walk to the Richard Rodgers Theater.

Cori didn't follow Broadway that closely, but when she saw the marquee, she gasped and turned to Micah. "Hamilton! We're seeing Hamilton? How did you get tickets?"

"I ordered them as soon as I had the first interview at the Landing. I figured if I didn't get the job, I'd come and use the tickets anyway."

"You ordered two tickets?"

"I was counting on you joining me."

"You didn't even know me."

"I hoped to from the first time I saw you at the Gathering." He was referring to the first glance between them at Laurel

Ledge's annual fall festival. Cori kissed him hard from the bottom of her momentarily seized-up heart.

The crowds were unreal. It was amazing they could move, but they worked their way through to the theater and arrived at their seats. They were none too early.

The show was fantastic. They couldn't stop debriefing, but at the same time, Cori wondered where they were walking and how they were going to get back to Laurel Ledge. She knew Micah had a plan, so she kept walking and remained engaged in animated conversation.

They arrived at Grand Central Station. The Metro North. Good choice. They had some cheesecake at Cheesecake Factory, purchased tickets, and boarded for home.

By this time, Cori was exhausted. She fell asleep on his shoulder and didn't wake up until the train pulled into the New Haven station. She was groggy until the frigid night air hit her. Now alert, she panicked. "How are we going to get the rest of the way to Laurel Ledge."

"A couple of men from the Landing left my car here for us."

"You thought of everything."

"I tried. The evening's not over yet."

"Yes, it is! It's 1:30 in the morning."

"Oh. It's not even Valentine's Day."

"Nope."

"No more romance."

They hugged and got in the car.

She hadn't wanted to fall asleep again, but she did. They were in front of her condo when she awoke for a second time.

"Oh. I'm sorry. I'm not very good company, am I?"

"The best, in fact."

"Thank you. And thank you for this perfect Valentine's Day. Everything was astonishing, breathtaking, superb, and just amazing. How did you think of it all? How did you manage to put it all together?"

"I took things that have been on my bucket list and ratcheted it up several notches by including the person I want to be with most."

"Thank you."

He walked her to her door. He kissed her long and hard.

She whispered, "It was perfect."

"Goodnight."

"Night."

Chapter 31

"So, how was it?" Cori had sleepily answered her cell without checking the caller ID. She recognized that it was Jessalyn after a split second that seemed much longer.

"Amazing. So stunningly amazing that it will be hard to explain."

"So, try," Jessalyn insisted.

"Here are a few words. Helicopter. Catskills. Bleeker Street. Hamilton. Metro North."

"What! Fill in the blanks, please."

Cori did.

"Wow. Just wow. And after all that, he didn't propose?"

"Oh my gosh. No!"

"You sound relieved. Did it cross your mind?"

"No. It didn't. I guess I am."

"Did you have fun?"

"I loved it."

"Then, what is the problem?

"It's still too soon. We need time. A lot more time. We need to be sure."

"You're not?"

"No. This was the first time we've been together without a disagreement."

"Couples have those."

"I know."

"You're still questioning whether you two are on the same page."

"Still waiting to see. So, how was the sleigh ride?"

"Micah was onto something. We haven't necked that much in ages. If this was a text, I'd say, G.O.A.T. And the dinner wasn't bad, either."

Cori laughed. Jessalyn was a gem. *Teenagers have a definite influence on the language.*

"Cori, I lost track of time. I must go. Talk to you again."

"Thanks for checking up on me."

She had put down the phone when Stewart's ringtone sounded. It had been so long, she forgot he had his own ring.

"Hello."

"Hey. Cori. What's up?"

"Not much. How about you?"

"I have some news. Do you have time to get together?"

"With you?"

"Is it that far-fetched?"

"No." She giggled. "That's not what I meant. It didn't come out right. Sure. When?"

"As soon as you can."

"Okay." She hesitated.

"You're wondering how what's-his-face will react."

She hesitated again. She couldn't lie.

Steward piped up. "Have him come."

"Is that okay?"

"If he's that important to you. Sure."

"Okay. We had a very late night. I'm just getting myself together."

That sounded way more serious than it should.

Stewart tried to act nonplussed and teased. "I see. Give me an estimate. I can arrange my day accordingly."

"It won't take that long. I'm just not thinking clearly. How about the café at Amity at 10:00 a.m.?"

"Perfect. See you then, and your friend too, if he wants."

She wanted to give Micah time to adjust his schedule and to prepare for the possibility of seeing Stewart, so she called him first.

"He didn't say why?"

"No."

"It's at Amity?"

"Yes."

"Okay. I'll see you then."

"Thanks."

Cori and Micah arrived first. They sat down and waited. Cori tried to make small talk. "How are you feeling this morning? I think I'm still in disbelief about such a wonderful evening."

"Until this development." Micah spoke softly but with disdain.

"Would you rather I had met with Stewart alone?" Cori was trying to mollify Micah's discomfort but wasn't effective.

"Or found out what it's about," Micah quipped.

"I'm sorry." Just then she spied Stewart.

He was a presence but didn't burst on the scene. "Don't get up. Anyone having coffee?" He looked confused. *Who wouldn't have a cup of coffee this time of the morning; especially after the night these two allegedly had?* "I'm going to get one. What can I get for you?"

"I'll come too." Micah reluctantly joined him. While walking he inquired. "You didn't say what this is about?"

"It's about Cori's adoption."

"You have news. I didn't know you were involved. She didn't tell me."

"She doesn't know. Let's wait and talk about it with her, okay?"

They got the coffees and headed back for their seats.

Cori smiled and said, "So? What's this about?"

"You gave Dr. Dallas permission to investigate your adoption, right?"

"Yes."

"His wife said it was okay to investigate on your behalf and seek permission from the woman who originally closed the file to share it with you. He did, and he hired me to help."

"Oh. Then you have something?"

"A lot. Brace yourself."

"Okay. I am."

Dr. Dallas delivered you. The birthdate on your certificate is accurate. Your birth mom found her way to Compass Points from New York City after escaping her employer. She was abducted and forced to work as a nanny, likely for one of the architects who participated in the Estonia Sovereignty Declaration of 1988. The family lived with him in New York where he came for training in one of the university institutes.

"Officially she was a nanny. But she was a slave. She didn't receive wages, time off, or any benefits. She was in tough shape when she arrived at Compass Points, and they took care of her until you were born. Dr. Dallas arranged through his wife to find a family for you.

"In those days, there were fewer services to help someone start over. Compass Points offered to help her look for a job and obtain a work visa, but she knew so little English it appeared there were too many obstacles. She was homesick and wanted to go back home. Contact with her parents, who couldn't afford to send her travel money, convinced them not to return her to Estonia right away. So, Compass Points scraped up some spending money and a plane ticket. It was a tough decision not knowing what they were sending her to.

"Anyway. We found her. She is married and living in Tallinn. That's sort of the Silicon Valley of Europe according to some people. Her husband owns a software company. Her name is Marga Oras Sittow. I met her Cori. And she wants to meet you."

The breath was knocked out of Cori. She listened with rapt interest, but his last two sentences stunned her. Her silence allowed Micah to speak.

"How do you know she wants to meet Cori? What did you do to ensure she is Cori's biological mom?"

"Officially, nothing yet. But her DNA is being tested. We'll have a comparison soon. She learned English in case her daughter found her someday." Stewart had tears in his eyes as well as his voice.

Micah had fire in his eyes. "Don't you think it would be a good idea to authenticate the relationship before getting Cori's hopes up?"

"That's up to Cori. I'm here to serve. I can take you to see her as soon as you're ready to go, or we can wait for DNA confirmation, or we can never go."

Cori still said nothing.

"Do you need time to think about it, Cori?" Stewart asked gently.

She looked at him and shook her head yes. "Do you have a picture, Stewart?"

He brought pictures of Marga when she was small, the day she was married, and now. "She has no children. I sensed it was her health, but it might have been anything."

"Why didn't she look for Cori?" Micah continued in his skepticism about the situation.

"Guilt. Guilt that convinces someone they are a nonentity. Believe me, she has grieved for Cori all of these years."

"What about her husband?"

Stewart hadn't met him. "He was traveling during the short time I was there. She texted him that I had arrived. I may have the wrong impression, but I think I'm right that he is supportive of her meeting Cori."

Cori was coming out of her stupor, though the situation still seemed surreal. She had wanted this for months. "I might want to go right away, if it's okay with Amity."

"I wish you would rethink this, Cori. At least wait for DNA confirmation." Micah was intent on slowing down the process.

"Micah, can you look at those pictures and have any doubt?"

"That doesn't always mean anything, Cori."

"I'll live with the consequences if she's not the one. She's someone I would like to meet, regardless."

The elephant in the room was any mention of Cori's biological father. Neither man brought up the subject, which left it to Cori.

"So, the man who begot me held my mother against her will while seeking the liberation of a country. If you're wondering if I want to meet him, or know more about him, or want to know what he looks like, or if I want to know if I have siblings, the answer is no. I would like to exercise my choice to have nothing to do with him."

That elephant evaporated, for the time being.

Stewart added sheepishly, "We actually don't know who your father is. Marga wouldn't talk about it with me, and she didn't tell Dallas either. She may have talked to her family about it, or her husband. But I doubt it. I suspect she has refused to talk about it with anyone."

Cori wanted to be alone with her thoughts. "Thank you, both. This will take a lot of processing. You both have helped. I'm going to call Roman, Claris, and Jessalyn. And, I'm going to check with Amity about the time off. Oh. No. More time off! Who should be in touch with Marga? She must be waiting to hear what we're going to do. We don't need visas, do we?"

"No. Your passport is enough. Just tell me what you want to do, and I'll text Marga. Here is her email address and telephone number for when the time is right for you to contact her. Maybe you'd prefer to video chat." Stewart was prepared for when Cori was ready.

Cori went to her office and called Roman, Claris, and Jessalyn. They all were encouraging of her pursuit. Micah was the only skeptic. She walked to Human Resources and explained the situation. She was told to submit a family leave request with the dates to be determined.

She went through the motions required by work for the time being. On occasion, she wondered if she was doing justice to the tasks, but she didn't know what else she could do.

Chapter 32

Forging a relationship with Marga was anything but natural. During the months of searching for the identity of the woman who had given her birth involved pushing for results. She had given no thought on how to define their relationship or where to begin. Marga wasn't much older than Cori, but she wasn't pursuing a friendship. Neither was the relationship with her adoptive mom a pattern for relating to Marga.

Thus, a millennial relationship ensued. How else but to email, snapchat, Facebook, and text. As eager as Cori was for information, she respected Marga's gentleness and tact in turning each communication around to gaining information about Cori. Marga wasn't just hungry for information, she was ravenous. Doubts that daunted Cori during her search never resurged. Marga cared.

It was a great challenge for Cori to discover any information about Marga's experiences in the United States. Marga talked about her involvement in her husband's business, their travel, and the times (though few) they spent relaxing in the resort town of Pirita.

At the close of their second video chat, Cori broached the subject again and gently pressed Marga for the information she knew was sensitive. Cori plied Marga's motherly sentiments toward settling her daughter's need to know her history. Cori acknowledged that it would be heart-wrenching for both and suggested that Marga take her time by writing it down in an email—structuring the prose with as many drafts as possible before hitting "send."

Thirty-six hours later, there was an email.

"We lived under the rule of the Soviet Union, and it was the only way of life I remember as a young girl. We were taught what the Supreme Soviet wanted us to know. They told us what songs to sing, what history to study, and to worship only Soviet leaders. If we wanted a Christmas tree, we had to hide it from windows or doors because anything or anyone could betray us.

"My parents told me about the real Estonia in whispers. I didn't know if my friends knew the same things I did because we didn't know whom we could trust. They told me about Estonian independence in the twenties and thirties. And about the Nazis and Russia making a pact, a pact that my parents told me was illegal. Anyone speaking out against the Russians, then the Nazis, and then the Russians again after the war were sentenced to hard labor.

"My father's family was sent to Siberia to work in the labor camps because my grandmother's brother was one of the Forest Brothers. The Forest Brothers were just as they sound. They lived in the forest and took every opportunity to sneak an attack on Russian soldiers. Or maybe it was because my great-aunt had literature not in line with the Soviet version of history in her classroom. But they didn't need a reason. My grandmother died in the labor camps from malnutrition and a broken body.

"My father and grandfather returned to Estonia, and my parents married in 1969. My grandfather died soon after I was born, and I don't remember him.

"The folk songs of my country were sung in my house softly to celebrate the old Estonia. There were many, many songs. But at our song festivals, which began more than a hundred years before I was born, we were made to sing about how wonderful the Soviets were.

"When I was a young teenager, Mikhail Gorbachev was in power. He hated how backward we were and announced that people could now have opinions and that countries under Soviet rule needed to have better market systems. But, after so many years of being careful about every word, it was difficult to trust. But we could sing. And we did sing.

"It was right after my graduation from school, and I was about to turn eighteen in the fall. There was a rally in the Old Town Square in Tallinn. There were speeches about Estonia's history. The flag of Estonia began to be waived by many people who had kept them hidden for many years. We began to sing the folk songs of Estonia, and we continued singing while marching to the festival grounds. This went on for two days. For the first time, we were hopeful. But then something happened that made me less hopeful than I ever had been before. I doubted that any of the new freedoms were true. That it was just more propaganda."

Chapter 33

Cori wanted to hear more but promised Marga she could take her time in getting to the rest of the story. She understood why Marga had bottled up the information for so many years. Cori video chatted immediately after receiving the email, and for the most part, they cried.

At Amity, Cori, half in jest, asked Blake if Amity contracted with an employee assistance program she could consult about her own issues. Her supervisor assured her that they would provide a service for her, all kidding aside. She promised to set it up.

Cori went by to see Claris, since it had been a few days. She filled Claris in on what she had learned so far. When she was silent, Claris gently dropped some information on Cori.

"Cori, because of our involvement in trafficking, we're going to investigate the circumstances surrounding Marga's abduction. I wanted you to know."

Aghast, Cori implored, "Why? There is no point now."

"I knew you and most of the world would feel that way. And so much has changed in Estonia since '88. But, just as a precaution, we want to look into the criminals who did this and what they're doing now."

Cori wasn't in a place to process information or form opinions. Sheepishly she mumbled, "Yeah. I guess that's good. Do what you can."

"We will."

What Claris didn't say was that they already were doing what they could. An attorney who served with Claris during her days in the New York District Attorney's office had contacted the federal attorneys' office for a probe, which was already underway. Claris hoped to have enough information by the time Stewart and Cori traveled to Estonia to accompany them for some in-country searches for the individuals involved.

* * *

Time had passed since Cori heard from Micah nor had she contacted him. She knew his opinion on this pursuit of hers, and she understood his need to protect her—though she viewed it as misguided. She texted him and asked if they could meet for lunch or for afternoon coffee. He texted back that it was good to hear from her; he had been out of town for a couple of days, and he would return on the following day. He asked about coffee the next afternoon, which was a Saturday, and she agreed.

Having imbibed way too much coffee in the last several days, Cori was trying to convert to green tea for her afternoon breaks. It wasn't growing on her as she had hoped, but she was determined to persist. Her edgy nature was enough without the added help of caffeine.

She was glad to see Micah, and they embraced. His voice was a bit hoarse as he whispered, "I needed that."

"Me too. Why did we wait so long?"

"Fear, I guess. That seems to be the cycle."

"Of me?"

"Of, yes, you and the unknown."

"Face your fears! Better yet, embrace them. They're in a human form that looks like me!"

"I'm trying." As they sat down, he hesitated. "Do I dare ask, how are things?"

She told him about Marga's message.

He ventured, "How are you?"

"Muddled. In pain, but less than I was."

He took a deep breath and stared at her.

"I know you hate to see me in pain. I've never gone through anything like this, but I've been through pain, Micah."

"Yes, and I want to spare you any more pain, if I can."

"I appreciate the sentiment. I need to make my own decisions about this. Your being there for me is important to me, but that is where your choice lies."

Another sigh. "Got it." There was a pause. "Do you know when you're leaving?"

"That leads to more information that I haven't told you. I'm glad we haven't made plans yet. Claris is hoping to find out about the family that abducted Marga. She and Trent plan to join us and look into their current status, if they can."

"That seems absurd after all this time, doesn't it?"

"I've blocked out what that might look like. I can't be concerned with it right now."

He turned away, deep in thought. Moments went by. When he spoke, his voice was hushed but imploring. "Cori, promise me you won't travel overseas until you have the DNA confirmation. You're already in this so deep."

"I think I can promise that. It makes sense to be sure. Maybe I won't be in so much of a daze by then."

"Thanks. That's such a relief." He then paused before saying, "Are we okay?"

"This is hard for everyone. I know that. Yeah, we're fine. But I'm not going to be any kind of 'fine' for who knows how long. I don't know how much other folks can put up with at this point. I guess that's something anyone around me will have to decide for themselves."

"Right. I'm in."

"I'm glad."

"I've not had time to prepare for tomorrow, so I'd better go. Will you be at the Landing for tomorrow's service?"

"Yes. I'm planning on it. The group is planning to go out for lunch after. I don't know how much the kids know. I've told Reina and Lottie the basics."

Micah stood and then kissed her quickly. He didn't break his gaze for several seconds after the kiss, and then left without saying anything else.

Chapter 34

Cori wanted to stay in bed and keep the curtains closed on Sunday, as if that could stop her racing thoughts. She dreaded what she needed most, which was being with friends. She had nothing to give, and she feared social situations when she was feeling so drained of an ability to interact with the banter required by a lively group.

The interactions of the day were effective in penetrating that fog for a short time, but the brooding returned soon after her return to her condo. She curled up on the sofa and watched live television. She had no idea what she was watching, but she was conscious enough to ensure it had no relationship to March Madness.

Work demanded her full attention on the following day, and she was on her way to a meeting about hiring additional counselors when she encountered Claris outside of her office. Claris asked if they could get together after work. Cori agreed and suggested her condo as the venue. As she proceeded to her meeting, she celebrated what had been more than a half day of respite from obsession with 'the situation.'

Claris texted that Stewart and Brent would be joining them, so Cori texted a group message that she would prepare an appetizer. She had fixings for a chef's salad on hand, which she threw together as soon as she arrived at home, after having stopped at a deli for the makings of salmon on toast tips. She changed into a long-sleeved, white-corseted tunic top and legging jeans and then warmed the toaster oven for the toast tips.

Stewart arrived first, and it wasn't the first time that her motor revved at the sight of his Dave Franco looks. She was accustomed to slowing the roll on those feelings. Sometimes it was almost impossible. He wore a variation of what he always wore, but somehow it seemed varied and attractive. Always jeans, an untucked shirt, and a slim-cut sport coat.

Stewart's stare enveloped her entire being signaling that his reaction matched hers. She could have included Micah in the evening but failed to follow through on inviting him. He would be interested in the news to be shared and any plans that might be made as well. But it was her intention to keep Micah and Stewart apart. *Why am I keeping them apart? Is it their reaction to one another or my reaction to Stewart?*

They were still enjoying their similar but individual rush of feelings when Trent and Claris appeared at the door, which had yet to be closed behind Stewart.

Greetings were followed by piling up plates and bowls and each taking a place on the sofas. Claris made a purposeful gesture to swallow and was the first to speak of the subject they knew was inevitable.

"Cori, we have some news. We have the name of the family that abducted Marga. It wasn't complicated given the timeline, first names of the wife and children, the nationality and the approximate address all provided by Marga. And, it has been confirmed by passport records from the U.S. State Department. We made contact with the U.S. Embassy in Estonia, and they were able to verify the information as well.

"The Embassy in Estonia has placed us in contact with the national police, and they are trying to locate the family."

Despite her declared disinterest in the spear side of her family, Cori found she was absorbed in what Claris had said and couldn't decide what follow-up questions to ask first. She blurted, "Do they think they can find them? Is prosecution possible, do you think?"

"Prosecution is not the major objective, so to speak. But they should be interrogated. We can't anticipate what information could emerge. I don't even want to conjecture. He was a Russian-speaking resident of Estonia, probably emigrated during the Soviet era. His wife was Estonian."

"No!" Cori objected with a combination of disappointment and disbelief.

"What, Cori?" Stewart was stunned about her change in mood and worried about her as well.

"That's wrong. We're on the wrong track!" Cori fumed.

"But why?" Claris was gentle out of concern and tried not to upset her further.

"Not Russian. I don't have Russian in my DNA!"

There was silence. No one doubted what Cori said. Instead, they were reviewing the facts to determine where things went south.

Trent contributed his first comment since this discussion began. "The three first names, the address, the nationality. I don't believe in that many coincidences."

"Then what?" Cori demanded. After all this time, she had her first doubt that Marga was her mother. *Micah was right. I shouldn't have dived in like this.*

Stewart was as upset as Cori, particularly for Cori. He felt responsible. He was tentative as he tried to reason through the mess in front of them. "Marga's DNA will be available anytime. That will settle the most important question. If Marga doesn't connect to Cori, you all are off the hook to pursue her story. I feel responsible to get her some answers. But I won't leave Cori in the lurch either. We'll go back to the drawing board and chase leads until we have answers."

No one wanted to say anything. Trent, though shaken, sensed he was impacted the least by the new information, and he took the lead. "I suggest that no one outside of this room be informed about our confusion. Can we agree?"

They all agreed. Claris was reluctant to leave Cori, but Trent convinced her they should be on their way. As they drove off the premises, Trent offered his opinion to Claris. "You know, by the late 80's, Russians represented forty percent of the Estonian population, up from eight percent at the beginning of the occupation. I don't think it's a stretch to think that the family was headed by a Russian. I suspect he came to the U.S. under the guise of studying and reforming market systems, but likely he was part of the Popular Front. They were the group that favored freedom within the Soviet system; not freedom from the Soviets."

"That's all feasible, but it doesn't explain what Cori said."

"I know. Whatever this means, I'm in this. I want answers for Cori and I want answers about this Russian, even if the two stories don't intersect."

"Me too."

Stewart and Cori were standing at the still-open door after the Trent and Claris send-off. He turned to her and was flooded with the heightened excitement he experienced whenever she was close. The sensual mingled with the increasing concern he felt for her situation. He reached out and pulled her close. He held her for a long time before releasing her and whispering, "Are you going to be okay?"

"One way or another, yes." She was deflated by the news but aroused by his embrace. She managed to form a sentence. "Don't worry about me. It's okay Stewart. This isn't on you, for crying out loud."

He didn't feel much better, but it still was good to hear her say it. They said good night avoiding any further eye contact.

* * *

Cori had said nothing to Micah about the plan to get together with the others on Monday, so he had no expectations about new information. They had coffee one day and went out for a dinner and movie one evening. Their times together should have been good distractions, but nothing seemed to capture her interest. That is until she received a follow-up email from Marga on Wednesday of that week.

"I am sorry for the delay in telling you the rest of the story. As I said, we were fearful and hopeful in Estonia at that time. I had taken part in the "Singing Revolution" a couple of times in the early summer of 1988. I am not political, but the hope of a restored Estonia was very emotional and made many of us braver. I was working as a lifeguard at a pool catering to families of government officials during that summer. I was hoping to earn my way to Tartu University eventually.

"I first saw the person who stole me from my parents during a session with very small children when he came to pick up his children. I might not have remembered him when he grabbed me on my walk home several days later except for the impression he left during that one time at the pool. He never made eye contact with his children, and they seemed frightened by him. He stared at me until he left with the children following behind him.

"He didn't just steal me, he attacked me. I lost consciousness, but I could tell when I woke up. He took me to his home. His wife, the mother of these children, never questioned who I was. I begged her to let me go home. I stopped when she struck me.

"We traveled soon. Until then, I was locked in the playroom. The mother, the children and I flew in a different section of the airplane. I didn't see the father. They had a passport for me and everything, but I never saw it. It was easy for them. My papers were in a file because of my job at the pool.

"Life in what I found out was New York was the same. I had a bed in a closet just off the large playroom. I took care of the children. Their meals were brought in and any educational instruction was my responsibility using materials they gave me. The materials were in our own language and had no clues as to where I was or how to get away.

"I didn't see the mother very often. This went on for weeks. Sometimes the mother would take the children out for a few hours. No one realized the little girl kept a souvenir brochure of one of their outings. It was a playbill that had a small, makeshift map on it, and I basted it into one of her teddy bears to hide it.

"I tried to plan my escape, but I couldn't think of anything. I decided it had to be when the mom was out with the kids, so I made my move soon after I found the map. I took the drawers out of a chest of drawers, braced it on its back between the sofa and the closed playroom door, threw a chair through a window, and climbed out. I used the chair to help me climb over the fence and onto the street.

"Studying the map helped me to understand streets and avenues. I could see I was at Forty-Seventh Street and Second Avenue. I could see Forty-Sixth, so I went in that direction as fast as I could and started to zig zag to Forty-Second Street. I ran to Broadway and found the church named in the brochure. Later, when I learned English, I realized that the church claimed to be the haven for Broadway stars. I kept the brochure and re-read it many times.

"The church protected me for just a couple of days but wanted to get me to a shelter away from the city. They took me to Compass Points. You were born a few months after I arrived. I will write more about this later.

"I called my parents, but we were afraid for me to return to Estonia until we were sure no one was after me. I asked distant cousins in Finland if I could live with them for a year. The doctor at Compass Points got me a duplicate passport.

"I didn't go back to Estonia until 1992. I was so happy to be back and to know they were going to have free elections that year. I had been part of the "Singing Revolution" even though I had given up hope that Estonia would ever be free.

"That is all for right now, dear Cori."

Cori could hardly read through her tears. Her sobs were audible as the reality finally dawned that she would never hear the details about her arrival in this world. For the first time she felt the brunt of the horror Marga endured as gruesome pain wracked her body ushering in a fleshly tribute to the brutal act she had suffered. Cori imagined that a psychotic break might be the best coping mechanism to make sense in such a barbaric situation. And Marga was barely out of her childhood. Cori sobbed for a long time for Marga and for herself.

When she had recovered enough to talk, she called Jessalyn. She confessed to what she had been hoping for and admitted it was a fool's errand to think she would ever hear a joyful recounting of her entry into this world. Jessalyn let her cry for a short period before offering a gentle correction. "The overflowing joy of an ecstatic mother at the sight of your arrival happened as surely as I am talking to you now. It was breathtakingly real and magical. It was on the face of Irene Sellers, and her elation was shared by an adoring congregation. I remember. I was part of that congregation."

Cori left the conversation more grounded and grateful.

Claris sent out a group text while Cori was talking to Jessalyn. She had heard the beeping but had chosen to ignore it. Claris wanted all of them in her office as soon as they could get there. Cori, of course, was first on the scene.

"Marga is your mother, Cori. There is no doubt." Claris was close to breathless as she nearly pushed the words on Cori.

Cori sat down and stared straight ahead. "Good." She gulped. "I'm relieved it's over."

"Me too."

"What does this mean about her attacker?" Cori muttered.

"I don't know." Claris had just finished her answer when Stewart knocked and entered. They filled him in. He rubbed his brow, blew out a long breath of relief, and then looked at both of his companions.

"We have to go over there." He blurted. "Sorry," he blurted again.

"Not sorry. I agree." Claris responded quickly.

"All four of us?" Stewart was skeptical.

"Yes." Cori avowed. Claris concurred. Trent arrived, and they caught him up to that point in the conversation. He agreed about the trip and left to search for an empty office to make reservations. When Stewart realized what Trent intended, he trailed after him.

Claris called the Attorney General's Office and asked for help in contacting high level law enforcement in Estonia. Her intended next step was to locate the Russian-speaking man, whose residence it was where Marga had been captive and interrogate him.

Cori felt relief and a little left out at the same time. Everyone seemed to have something to do but her. Soon, the guys returned. She doubted they could have made plans already and quizzed them on the latest. "What's up?"

"Stewart warned me that travel to Estonia is a tad disjointed. The most frequent flights are through Moscow, of all things." Trent seemed baffled. "We have to be willing to travel through there or not leave for a week or even two!"

"I know we're anxious to get to the truth, but maybe we can slow this down a bit." Stewart was attempting to be the voice of reason, which was not his typical role in the cast. "The immediate need has been met—to find out who is Cori's mother. We know that already."

"Right." Suddenly Cori seemed far more settled. "Right! I want to meet Marga, but it doesn't have to be right now. In fact, it might be better to have the "internet relationship" for a while before we get up close and personal. And I've tried not to care about my father. I'm curious for Marga's sake to better understand her sordid story, but that may or may not happen. So, where does that leave you guys?"

Trent appeared to exercise restraint, but he couldn't pull it off. "Ever since becoming involved in intervention, I guess I'm anxious about immediacy. Claris and I have discussed ad nauseum if there's anything legal we can do about this situation. It's a possibility. There really is no statute of limitations. Perhaps more a limitation on active interest.

"That would simply provide an indictment. Rendition, or extradition, is another issue. It depends on cooperation from Estonia."

Cori inquired further. "So, Trent, what do you hope to accomplish?"

Trent shook his head and shrugged his shoulders. "It may sound naïve, but what if whoever was involved has repeated it or grown the operation? I want to find out what we can."

"I feel you, man. I'll help." Stewart was no longer putting on the brakes. "What's our next step?"

"Let's wait to see if Claris can get a bead on where the New York City D.A.'s office stands, and if there's no pulse there, let's pursue the Feds. If that fails, we can reach out to Estonia ourselves."

"But we can do most of that from here, right?"

"Yeah. You're right. Let's get something to eat. We'll leave word with Claris where we plan to be. How's that sound?"

Chapter 35

Cori, Stewart, and Trent were sharing tomato bruschet-ta with a balsamic glaze when Claris arrived. Once again breathless with news, she told the group about her call to the New York City D.A.

"They gave me the name of the Russian-speaking dude. He's Ilia Papanov. He's Russian born but lived most of his life in Estonia and was married to an Estonian, as we already know. Her name is Evelin. He's what we would call semi-retired. They first reported he was in a government resort in Anapa on the Black Sea, then corrected themselves to say he was in Moscow. Their last information indicated he's back in Tallinn on an as-signment. They don't know for how long. They're going to try to arrange for us to ask questions. We have no rendition treaties with Russia, so we may have a short window before he returns there."

Cori was trying to feel distant from the news, but she was far more interested than she thought she should have been.

The appetizer was filling, so they skipped the entree and shared a couple of desserts before saying good night. The plan was for Claris to summon them together again when she had news.

Claris and Trent had arrived separately. Cori drove to The Landing to look for Micah, whom she wanted to tell about the confirmed DNA match. Claris said she had some work to complete and returned to the office. Left alone, Trent and Stewart mulled over what they saw as their options. Each acknowledged they felt all over the place about what they should do. They were landing on nothing when Stewart decided to get radical. "I'm going to go long here. Let's not give this creep time to relocate. I don't want to involve you in an irregular rendition, so let's get over to Estonia while the getting is good."

"Let's make the reservations as soon as we can."

They went back to Claris's office to run it by her and hit up against the same problems as before. Flights through Moscow are possible right away, but it was a long poke. If a flight was delayed, they didn't want to exceed the 24-hour window that might require a visa to hang out in Moscow, and it would be more complicated if they needed to leave the airport. It would take days to get connections through other cities.

"I'm out." Trent was out of steam. It had been over an hour of experimenting with options that didn't seem to work, so they decided to pack it in for the night.

They were just about to shut off the lights to Claris's office when Cori's ringtone sounded on Stewart's cell.

"Hey Cori. What's up?"

"I think you should go to Tallinn right away before Papanov changes locations. I can imagine there are plenty of people who would be willing to leak information to him and make him jumpy."

"Yeah. We thought the same things. Nothing pops as a good travel plan."

"That's really why I called. Marga said her husband flies to cities in Europe a lot. She suggested trying Stockholm, and he could pick you up there."

"That could work! We're gonna try again. I'll call you back."

They booked a flight for the next day and texted Cori. Cori in turn emailed Marga, and Marga set it up for her husband, Taavet, to meet their flight.

When her pace slowed enough to consider all that had happened, she realized Dr. Dallas could have traced Marga's captors by way of passports since Marga had one and had entered the country legally. She needed to find out why he didn't.

* * *

Claris and Cori were left behind. Cori's visit to Marga was a definite plan for the near future, but she didn't envy anything Stewart and Trent were about to do. Claris agreed that only one lawyer was necessary, so she stayed back and tried to keep up with the task force and Amity assignments for the time being. It wasn't far from her mind that a trip to the New York D.A. might be needed.

Cori had made plans for later in the week with her young friends and left her condo for a short time to pick up some supplies in preparation. The project this time was going to be a movie matinee followed by homemade spaghetti.

As she approached the door to her condo, she noticed someone hanging outside on the terrace. She stared in disbelief as the individual approached her and she became aware that it was Simone. She hadn't spoken to or even seen Simone since the accidental encounter at the Briny Bluffs resort where Cori had always spent Thanksgiving getaways with Simone's tribe. Cori believed Simone when Simone lied about cancelling the family gathering, which turned out to be a ruse to keep Cori from going. It had backfired.

The past rushed over Cori's thoughts allowing Simone to speak first. It was tentative. "Hey. I know you're surprised by my coming here."

Cori nodded her head in the affirmative, eyebrows raised. "Understatement."

"I'm sorry for what happened. I won't go into a long explanation."

"Good. Let's not. It matters, but it also matters that we can be on to good things despite the past."

"Yeah. True. I've been meaning to say something sooner. I also wanted your help on something."

"My help? Look, come in. I'll put this stuff away."

She opened the door and offered Simone a seat. Instead, Simone followed her as far as the kitchen island and stood while Cori put away groceries. "Would you like coffee?"

"Only if you're having some."

Cori made coffee for both and didn't say anything more than offering Simone a seat at the counter. Simone finally sat down. "I have some information I hope you can help me make sense of."

"Okay."

"It's about Compass Points. Actually, it's about Dr. Dallas."

Not only did she have Cori's attention, Cori was gab blasted. She tried not to show it.

"A girl in my group at church came to me in a panic about her cousin, who is probably a nominal cousin only. This cousin was on the streets and wanted out of her lifestyle. The girl I know would have preferred to take her in but didn't dare to ask her folks. She knew a little about Compass Points and told her cousin to go there. The cousin did go, was treated well including medical tests and good food. She said most of the professional contact was with Dr. Dallas, who wasn't inappropriate with her. But she tried to tell Dr. Dallas about the guy who was her pimp, and it seemed to fall on deaf ears. She asked if she should go to the police, and he encouraged her to return home and focus on being a normal adolescent. There was still time to get over what she had been through."

Cori asked questions at this point. "Do you know where she was on the streets and where she was from?"

"Yeah. She was from a small town in Rhode Island and was looking for a big town experience in Hartford. He lured her, guess what, over the internet. "

"Did she go home?"

"Yeah. That's what the girl I know said. She's sure the cousin will bolt again. The girl I know is savvy and thinks it's way off that this wasn't reported. Her cousin is only sixteen."

"It is off. This might go better with names, if that's okay?"

"Yeah. The girl in my group is Enora; 'cousin' is Keelan. No rhyme intended."

It was a shadow of Simone's wit, but it brought back momentary good memories. There had been so many of them.

"Do you think we can talk to Keelan?"

"I think so."

"What is the best way to approach her, through Enora? Or do you think that's putting her in an uncomfortable position?"

Simone chuckled. "Wait until you meet Enora. She's the real deal. Her peers think she's a little 'extra,' but she's definitely worth it." Another short giggle.

"Simone, why did you come to me?"

"I heard things. Things about you and Compass Points."

"I'm glad I know this information on Dallas. I've been back and forth on him and his reputation. I think I'm more back than forth right now."

"What do you think should happen?"

"It all depends on what we find out. Minimum he should be slapped with a fine if he didn't report it. He's a mandated reporter. Creep."

"I'd better go. I'll let you know what Enora finds out."

"Yup. I have a date with some young friends tomorrow late afternoon through dinner. Nothing planned beyond that."

Cori called Claris as soon as Simone left. Claris's response was comical.

"You live a charmed life, Cori."

Cori laughed and said she would be in touch as soon as all involved were ready to meet at the Office of the District Attorney in Hartford, which she asked Claris to set up for her.

Chapter 36

Watching the last Spider-Man movie with the girls was fun, and the girls were lively as usual. Louise suggested they take a group selfie in front of the movie poster and further encouraged Cori to send it via Snapchat. One look at the picture and Louise declared, "We sure were cheesin'! Except for Della. Cori, you should post hashtag 'squad goals' by the picture."

Della piped up, "Oh, that is so last year."

Louise responded in kind with, "That's so last decade!"

Della bested her with, "Good clap back." They all laughed.

Cori had delivered the last girl home when Stewart's ringtone interrupted her drive. She pulled into a parking lot in time to answer.

"Hey Cori. How are things?"

"I can't say they're boring, but I'll elaborate another time. I can't wait to hear your report."

"We contacted Papanov right away, and he's going to meet with us tomorrow. He insists on meeting at the Embassy. I hope that isn't a bad sign. At least there will be an interpreter."

"Do you think he plans to lawyer-up?"

"Entirely possible."

"That would be a bummer. Hey, it must be, what, about 1:00 a.m. there?"

"About."

"Thanks for the update. Don't you think you should be getting some sleep?"

"Yeah I do. Just wanted to let you know. I'll call again when we have more news."

"Thanks. Sleep well."

Cori was about to start the car when she heard her texting signal. She sat back and opened the text, which was from Simone.

"Enora said Keelan will meet with us any day, but after school."

Cori texted back. "Let's have her on deck for tomorrow. Let her know we'll pick her up at 3:00 p.m. Address?"

"Will do. I'll meet you in Amity's parking lot at 1:00 p.m.?"

"Yup. Does she know we have to drive back to Hartford?"

"Yup. She can spend the night with me if she needs to."

"That's good of you. Be in touch if things change."

"K."

She called Claris to see if 5:00 p.m. would work with the Criminal Division of the Hartford D.A.'s office. Claris said she would make it happen.

* * *

Cori felt like a slacker both in her commitment to The Landing and to Micah. She was letting their relationship fade. It had happened gradually, and she was at the point where it would feel better to endure the embarrassment of contacting him rather than to keep feeling the gnawing guilt. She took the high road and placed the call.

"Hi. Cori. It's good to hear. Are things okay?"

"Yeah. Ever new. If you want to hear, I'd love to talk."

"Sure, I want to hear. What works?"

"This morning?"

"Sorry. I can't during the day. How about this evening?"

"This is an awful thing to ask, but I'll be busy until at least 8:00 or 9:00 p.m. Too late?"

"No. Of course not. I'll be in the office working. Just text. Even if it can't work out, just let me know."

"Good. I look forward to it."

* * *

She and Simone had quite a conversation on the way to collect Keelan. The relationship was stilted, especially at first. Cori wasn't interested in backtracking to process what happened between them but focused on the common interests they had shared in the past. The frosty atmosphere broke up a bit. A discussion, understand sometimes an argument, about crime dramas ensued—a common interest to both.

Cori was insistent in her opinion of the best crime drama ever, "I just don't know how you could say there was a better show, that's all I'm saying. I loved the plot twists, the characters, the humor, and the way she outsmarted the bad guys. I hate long story arcs, and I don't like lawsuits either, but the way the writers crafted the lawsuit against her based on the way she solved her cases was genius. And her lawyer's reactions to her were side-splitting. Especially when he watched her 'do her thing' while interviewing a suspect. Do you remember? 'And there it is,' he said when she pulled one of her dubious deceptions."

Simone was conciliatory, for a moment. "I replay that episode at least once a year. It's mint. But I don't think I can agree with you that an outdated show is the best crime drama. Think of all of the different media outlets and all they have to offer."

"Don't even talk to me about the ones that drop the 'F-bomb' every two seconds. I can't join the discussion since I've never watched one for more than ten minutes."

"I'm not talking about those necessarily. But I can watch them and ignore the language. And what about all of the legal dramas and the ones with political overtones?"

"You mean the ones where the audience is manipulated from gasping at the newest murder to rooting for the murderer within a few episodes? I can't stand being 'handled' like that."

"It is genius writing, though. You have to admit that!" Simone opened her mouth to stage an additional comeback but clammed up when she noticed they were nearing their destination. She was left with the thought that Cori often argued in absolutes.

The GPS was accurate, and they found Keelan with no trouble. Keelan's mom was there to provide permission for the trip but wasn't interested in accompanying them. The strain between mother and daughter was obvious. One of the first comments Keelan made when they were settled in the car was, "Probably you don't like how salty I am with Mom?"

Cori was driving, so Simone fielded the comment by assuring Keelan that they weren't in the business of judging mother-daughter relationships. "They're all tricky at best!"

Keelan responded, "Yeah. Most old ladies are all drake no matter what you do."

Cori didn't need to google the vocabulary so far but felt it could reach that point except for the fact that she was driving. She was reminded of Simone's giftedness with teens. With a very brief sentence as a prompt, Keelan embarked on a monologue about her movie choices.

"There really isn't a comparison between Marvel and DC movies in my opinion. I do like the animated DC movies okay, but not that much. My sister liked *"Suicide Squad,"* but she couldn't say why. She's right though. It had its good points. Doesn't it seem like plots in DC movies seem like all the same? They cram as much as they can into their plots to catch up to Marvel. You can tell that's what they're doing.

"Spiderman Homecoming was really good. Once in a while Marvel has such a good villain in the newer movies. The only good villain in the old Marvel movies was Loki. Actually, a lot of companies are trying to replicate Marvel. The best Marvel so far, though, is *Black Panther*. Or maybe *Thor: Ragnarok*. I saw that with friends, and we laughed our guts out."

She went on to talk about her views on the newer Star Wars movies and how, in her opinion, they're inferior to the older versions. "I think that's what happens when Disney owns everything."

Keelan proved to be a formidable witness. Though chatty and tangential at times, much like her explanation of movies, she had an astute memory for faces, names, dates, event sequences, and describing the horrible ways she was violated, though her vocabulary was right out of the urban dictionary. She also was clear on Dr. Dallas's lack of response to her reports. Keelan had insisted that her "homies," also known as Simone and Cori, be present for the interview.

Cori texted Micah that she was too wiped to get together, and she would explain later. She drove Simone and Keelan to Simone's car at Amity and said good night. Just as they pulled onto the street, Cori watched in horror as their car was rear-ended and shoved off the road onto the shoulder. The rear car reversed and sped off.

Cori grabbed her cell and snapped a picture but paid no attention to whether the picture was clear. Instead, she cleared the camera and dialed 911 as she rushed to check on Simone and Keelan.

Airbags had deployed, Keelan was swearing a blue streak, and Simone was trying to settle the chaos to no avail. Cori arrived and cautioned them to take stock of physical symptoms before trying to extricate themselves.

Cori tried to calm Keelan. "Keelan, just hush so that we can find out where you're hurt." Cori tried to aid in examining for injuries. Simone admitted she felt sore all over, presumably from the air bag. But who could tell? They were about to figure out a way to disentangle when the police arrived followed by an ambulance.

She left them in the hands of the medical professionals as the police peppered her with questions. She gave them the car's description, as best she could, and then said, "Let's check my cell and see if the picture helps."

The picture wasn't clear, but it would prove at least a bit helpful. The sector car radioed a description and asked if he could text the picture from her phone to get a "be on the look-out" to local and state authorities.

Simone and Keelan agreed to be checked out in the ER, and Cori said she would catch up with them. Though Simone's car could be driven, the police towed it to their evidence garage for forensics.

Cori called Micah from the ER, and he was at her side almost immediately. The more haste she brought to her attempt to fill him in on Keelan and Simone, the faster agitation mounted in his demeanor.

"Cori, isn't the emotional anguish you've brought on yourself for the last several weeks enough, you've added this level of danger to your life as well?"

Cori blocked out his response and focused on chatter about Simone, Keelan and how to support them. Keelan informed her mom of the assault, and her mom didn't take the news well. She long ago realized she wasn't the one in charge, however. Her anger had very little impact.

After a long night, or most of the night, Simone and Keelan were cleared medically, but told to see a doctor if any of their symptoms worsened. They walked slowly; both were sore, but nothing was broken.

Cori was worried about their safety. Micah was conflicted. He wanted to help and felt guilty about his outburst. "Why don't Simone and Keelan stay in the staff quarters of the Landing? There's onsite security, and if I transport them, they're far less likely to be discovered by the elements who sought to hurt or intimidate them."

Cori was touched by Micah's kindness and wouldn't allow herself to acknowledge the chiding he leveled at her earlier. He could see she looked relieved. Before she said anything in response, he had another suggestion. "Cori, let's ask security if someone will walk you to your car. I've parked at the visitors' entrance, and that isn't where onlookers will expect to find Keelan and Simone to leave the building, so that's a good thing. But it means I can't walk you to your car."

Cori complied and thanked the security guard as she entered her car. She parked in the designated carport at her condo and proceeded to the condo. A shadow appeared and startled her. When she realized it was Dr. Dallas, she was outright frightened. Saying nothing, she attempted to walk around him with her head down. He grabbed her arm and gruffly spoke. "What do you think you're doing? I helped you. And you do this to me?"

"We can discuss this in my office. Call me there tomorrow. Let go of my arm." Cori tried to pull away.

Dallas increased his grip and pulled her back. "Don't do this. It isn't smart to mess around with me or any of these characters. Who do you think you are?"

Cori tried to walk away, but he held onto her. She was desperate to come up with a move when headlights from another resident's car shined on them, and Dallas released her. She said nothing, but ran to her condo, opened the door, entered and locked the door—including the deadbolt.

She rushed to the landline and called the Laurel Ledge police. Breathlessly she pushed out an explanation of what happened as coherently as she could manage. "This is Cori Sellers. I was a witness to an assault with an automobile at 945 Shoal Street earlier this evening. I was just detained outside of my residence by someone involved. I broke free when another car pulled into my condo complex. I'm at 286 Ridge Lane."

"Okay. If you want to press charges for assault, you can go to District Court and swear out a complaint on Monday morning at 8:30. The address is 223 Sill Street."

"You don't understand. There will be a court case that is more serious than the automobile assault. This is related."

"Hold on. I'll let you talk to the desk sergeant." He gave the impression this was a hand-off rather than believing there was merit to her comment.

"Sergeant Foley. Can I help you?"

"Thank you for taking my call, Sergeant Foley. My name is Cori Sellers. I was a witness to an assault on a motor vehicle by another motor vehicle this evening. The victims and I were returning from providing a statement to the Hartford Crime Prevention Unit about a prostitution ring. When I returned to my condo, I was accosted outside and prevented from entering my condo until another resident arrived in the parking area." She took a breath.

"Do you know who held you against your will?"

"Yes. Dr. Dallas. He is peripherally involved."

"As a perp?"

"As someone who knew what was going on and did nothing about it."

"Did he say anything in addition to holding you against your will?"

"Yes. He told me not to do this, among other things."

"Intimidating a witness is a felony. A detective from the night watch will be over to take a statement. Is that okay with you?"

"Yes. Thank you. Please have them show their shield at the door. I'm a little unhinged right now."

"You got it."

Detectives Skye Davis and Miles Prentice appeared within the half-hour. As requested, they showed their credentials, and Cori let them in. She repeated what had happened and described the players and events leading up to her encounter with Dallas.

Davis looked askance at Cori and asked, "What did Dallas mean after what he had done for you?"

Cori explained as succinctly as she could about his involvement in her birth, adoption, and eventually revealing what he knew about it."

"Why do you think he told you about your birth mother?"

"I don't know. I had accused him of being my father. Perhaps it was that and I was asking too many questions. For the time being, the information occupied me and kept me from suspecting anything more."

Detective Davis never changed expressions during Cori's attempt at an explanation. When Cori finished, there was a pause and then a sound that conveyed bewilderment. "Huh. Well, we're going to see what Dr. Dallas has for an explanation. We'll see if he's willing to talk without a warrant. Or we'll get a warrant. Not that you should know, but can you guess where we can find him?"

"My guess would be his office at Compass Points. He may have some records he wants to work on." Cori raised her voice inflection at the end of her sentence and her eyebrows to show her cynicism.

"Good point. I'd rather pick him up there than at his home anyway. Never a good thing to try to talk to someone with a lawyer in the house." Davis winked at Cori and then nodded at Prentice to get going. They were about to leave when Davis turned again to Cori, "We'll let you know."

Cori slept for a couple of hours, and then called Claris as well as the investigator in the Hartford Crime Prevention Unit. Cori remained agitated. She was frustrated that she hadn't gotten a look at the driver. She decided to go to work where she could be around people and begin to sort out her next moves.

Micah appeared in her office almost simultaneous with her arrival. She kissed him on the cheek and thanked him for being there for her. He hung his head low, put his hands in his pockets, and took a deep breath. "I'm sorry that I can't be more supportive."

"You are. Thank you so much for harboring Simone and Keelan."

"It's okay, but now what? Clearly, they don't want to take up residence there. How are they or anyone else going to ensure their safety?"

Cori was loath to keep information from him, but she couldn't quite decide to tell him about Dallas at this point.

"Keelan was very clear on who was her pimp. She's a good witness, Micah. She knew a lot of the characters by face and name. It's a matter of time until they are arrested, if not already."

"Probably all lackies in a ring that is beyond the reach of any branch of law enforcement. Cori, do you ever count the cost?"

She didn't know how to answer. She wasn't angry at him, per se. It was more that she was numb, perhaps stunned. Her only move was to turn away and think. But she couldn't think. She spoke without thinking through what she was about to say.

"It appears Dr. Dallas has known about any number of girls and women who have been victims of garden-variety and not so garden-variety perpetrators for over thirty years. He helped them with their health concerns and encouraged a safety plan, but he turned a blind eye to the culture of captivity surrounding the victims. I can't do that. I won't do that. Even if it means my life."

"Cori. Don't be rash just because you're upset with me."

"That's not it. I think you helped me to see the trajectory I am on."

"Then change it. The cops will do what little they can. And it will be pitifully little, probably. And they have more resources than you do. They'll get along without you."

"Maybe on this case, but there are others. And I know I need training, obviously. Plus, I don't intend to be part of interdiction and prevention. I want to be there for victim support."

"You're digging yourself deeper, and I'm afraid it's in reaction to my fears. I don't want to leave, but I will before I cause you to become more entrenched."

"Micah. I . . ."

"I'll be in touch. Keelan and Simone can stay as long as they need to."

Claris interrupted. She didn't apologize. "Keelan's pimp was picked up and charged with anything that applies to luring Keelan into selling herself for sex. The others Keelan named will be brought in as they are located. They want the kingpins. If they can flip any of them for the higher-level perps, they will. But it doesn't mean the bottom of the food chain will be released any time soon."

"Dallas?" It was Micah who asked. Cori stared at him and then at Claris for her response.

"He has been taken in for questioning. I have a warrant for his records, and I need help. Are you up to it, Cori? We will observe while the staff redact client names and assign case numbers. Names will be revealed of any who were under age, and the subpoena may be revised to include any who were victims of crimes. We're still reviewing the laws."

Micah looked defeated. Cori stammered. "I'm not a lawyer."

"If you'll join the task force, you can be cleared to help."

"I will. Where do I sign?"

"Come to my office right away. And, I have other news. Stewart has been trying to reach you. Is your phone off?"

"No. I don't think so." She checked. It was dead. She wasn't functioning as well as she wanted to pretend. Micah and Claris saw through her failure with the cell.

"Trent and Stewart had a long interview with Ilia. He's a creep. But, because of the events set in motion by Marga's escape, Ilia's wife was found to be having an affair with one of the security agents that had traveled with them from Estonia. It's likely he was the one who molested Marga—in fact abducted her in the first place. Ilia claimed he didn't know Marga was being held against her will. What a lousy excuse for a human being.

"Anyway, the family and crew returned to Estonia after Marga escaped. Ilia divorced his wife and got custody of the kids. They are grown and living in Russia. The wife and lover were killed in a small plane crash a couple of years after the divorce. Not that I am concerned about them, but if I could muster up concern, I'd investigate the circumstances of that incident. What a bunch of rotten people.

"Trent and Stewart are planning to talk to Marga today . . . probably already have. They'll let us know. Even with everything going on here, you'll want to check in with Marga after she finds out the truth about the family and her attacker."

Cori found that her legs weren't support enough for her, and she sank into her desk chair. Claris and Micah stared at her not knowing what to do. It seemed so trite to ask her for the umpteenth time if she was okay. Even though she said she didn't care about the biology of the male who attacked her mother, finding out about his story and death had its impact. So, they provided silence.

Eventually she rose and spoke rather matter-of-factly. "Well, I guess all that remains is to continue getting to know Marga. Regarding Estonia, I mean. Let's proceed with the Laurel Ledge case. Where did you say I should sign?"

Claris threw Micah a wary look and said, "My office Cori."

They made a move not knowing what Micah would do. Cori turned to him, "Thanks for helping Keelan and Simone. I'll come by and drive them home when I'm finished in Claris's office."

He cleared his throat and sheepishly said, "I'll see you then."

He moved passed them and was almost out of Cori's office when Cori made an ill-fated attempt at teasing him. "Micah. Are you at all happy that Simone and I are repairing our relationship?"

"Be careful what you wish for, right?" He turned to look at her with a defeated look on his face, then turned again to go.

Paradoxes.

Chapter 37

Cori and Claris felt buried in paper. There was no glamour in reviewing the Compass Points records, but it yielded copious amounts of information. Follow up would have to extend to many municipalities, states, and even overseas to investigate enterprises represented by the reports from victims who had found refuge at Compass Points. Claris and Trent could be headquartered in Laurel Ledge for a long time attempting to follow up.

Trent returned to Laurel Ledge during the time Cori and Claris were still shifting through the records at Compass Points. He went directly to the Amity Café and texted Claris and Cori to ask if they could join him. They were happy to see him and to get away from the drudgery of the volumes of files.

Cori, of course, mined all the information he could offer on Marga. Cori had plans to spend Easter in Estonia, both in Tallinn and at the beach in Pirita.

Cori also was curious about Stewart. Claris turned to Trent, and said, "Yeah. Where is Stewart?"

"He flew as far as Newark with me, and then said he had business in Pennsylvania. He rented a car and took off right away. He didn't say anything else about it."

Cori thought that sounded familiar. It reminded her of Ava. But it could be nothing. It was Stewart. He could be working on anything, including an extraction.

Trent looked like he had more to add. Claris noticed too. "What? I know you have something on your mind."

"It probably means nothing." Trent seemed to doubt himself.

"This is Stewart. It means something." Claris said it; Cori was thinking it.

"I heard part of a cell conversation with Lani Richards, the FBI agent, I'm quite sure."

"This has to be about Tashkent and the power plant, don't you think? Pennsylvania is where the firm is that hired the consultants. At least, that's where Ava was headed after we landed in Newark." Cori had no other information than that, but she was willing to bet there was a connection.

"Stewart was sure that Neil Reynolds tipped off the police in Tashkent about Stewart's rescue of the captive women. I wonder if he has information?" Claris hadn't told anyone this since it was only a hunch.

"The hotel safe! How could I be so scatterbrained! We didn't have time to scour the documents. Do you know if the Embassy looked at them?" Cori looked at Claris as she asked.

"I don't recall anything about documents. What were they?"

"Everything we could grab. Engineering designs, energy output data, handwritten notes, financial reports, downloads from the plant server—that sort of stuff. Stewart learned a ton of information just from what we were able to look at during the session with the engineering consultants."

Claris was on the move as she responded, "I'll check with the Embassy."

Trent added, "Stewart went back to the hotel. Would he have retrieved the documents?"

"I don't think so. I paid extra for a separate safe and set up a password no one else knows." Regret showed in her tone.

"We need to get our hands on it. First, I'll text Stewart to tell him we're on to him and see what he knows. I wouldn't put it past him to have cracked the password."

"Doubt it." Cori muttered the comment to herself.

Trent sent a text.

"Are you on your way to the Key Construction Solutions? Did you get the papers from the Xi'an hotel safe? How can we help? Call."

Trent's cell rang almost immediately. "Stewart?"

"It's me. You figured out what I was doing?"

"Cori did that."

"I should have known. Yeah. Reynolds is involved in this. I have proof, but I can't use it, and I don't want to involve you of all people."

"I'll ask no more questions except think twice about what you're planning to do. Oh, and about the safe at the hotel in Xi'an."

"I forgot all about it, man."

"It might be what you need. Is there anyone in Xi'an you trust?"

"Hard to say for sure. I trust Zhang Bao, who speaks very little English and Li Jie, who knows English well, even though he uses as few words as possible!"

"I think we need to reach out to them. And I hope you'll wait before doing anything with, or to, Reynolds."

"I'll give it a few hours. I want to get him in his office before the end of the day." Stewart was pumped, and it was hard for him to ratchet it down.

Trent reassured him, "You'll hear from us. Don't do anything until you do."

"I'll text you their cell numbers."

Claris had returned. "I left a message. I don't know the chances of hearing back from the Embassy."

Cori had been mulling over what she remembered from the past and what was happening before her. "I doubt Reynolds faxed anything to them. When I sent him to fax the information, I hadn't given him the number. He never asked; I noticed the omission and gave it to him. He had no intention of sharing those documents with the authorities. It's a good thing I took them to the safe. He would have destroyed them."

Claris wanted to grasp as many details as she could. "So, why would he let the group review the documents in the first place?"

Cori was confident of the answer. "He had no control over the volume of documents that were gathered once we arrived. As I think back, he stayed as close to the document review as possible. In fact, every chance he could, he gathered up a bunch and held onto them. He was holding most of them when I asked him to fax them to the Embassy. I'm sure he never bargained for someone like Stewart who noticed and memorized things such as monetary denominations and longitude and latitude notations. Come to think of it, I think Reynolds was behind re-calling the accountant, who originally was asked to be part of the team from Amity. Luckily Stewart picked up on some of the accounting discrepancies."

Trent, still, was cautious. "Let's see if we can get some proof before Stewart does something rash."

Cori moaned, "Stewart is always going to do something rash."

Claris offered to be in touch with Jie and Bao, and Cori gave her the password, "wordlessbook." Cori returned to her office.

"Hey, Cori. How's it going?" She had dialed Stewart's cell as soon as she returned to her office, and that's how he answered.

She responded with her teeth clenched. "What are you doing?"

"Nothing at all, apparently." He mocked. "I've been told to stand down."

"What do you have on Reynolds, and how did you get it?"

"I don't want you to be complicit."

"Spill it."

"Let's say I met someone who helped me find some tidbits I needed. Got me access to phone records for the police station outside of Tashkent not to mention ads on the dark web. The phone records are undeniable; Reynolds tipped them off in Tashkent. It's obvious he didn't leave China when he said he did and knew everything that was going on."

"Who helped you? Did it have anything to do with Taavet and his company?"

"I plead the Fifth. I've been on the dark web, but not this deep. This man's a genius."

"What did you find on the dark web?"

"I have airports, salon locations, and some IP addresses . . ."

"Why not give it to the FBI? That's more than one extractor can deal with. Even you."

"Thank you, I think. Hey, you've seen how much help they've been."

"They saved you in Uzbekistan and Kazakhstan. Have you forgotten?"

"That, they are good for. But listening to me? We'll see. I left some information with Lani Richards, but I'm not depending on them."

"You did the investigating for them. Turn it over."

"I can't turn over the phone records. I can't reveal how I obtained them. The locations are great, but I want names. I was going to pressure Reynolds to see a future in helping a little. The Feds have some locations. They don't know the details about Reynolds yet."

"You can't offer him anything. You need prosecutors."

"I can hook him up. I can do things the Feds can't."

"That scares me more than anything."

"I'll be in touch. How's Micah?"

"I think he's okay. We're not together right now."

"Ya', huh? Hope you're okay about it. But, that being the case, I'm in love with you. See you soon. Bye."

Cori looked at her cell as if it were an animate object. She whispered to herself, "What just happened?" A random thought came to mind. *Reynolds can't know the entire contents of the safe. Those files are from several players.* Cori sent a group text to the other three.

Stewart's ringtone sounded on Cori's cell, and he started speaking as soon as Cori picked up. "You're as much a genius as your stepdad. Whoops. I mean—anyway, all I need is a pile of printed papers, and I can fake it as if I have legitimate information on Reynolds."

"Why couldn't you let the Feds pressure him?" Cori was desperate.

"We've been over this. The cell call to the police is the only thing I have on him. I told you, I can't give that to the Feds. But I gotta get some names from Reynolds."

"How do you know Reynolds hasn't skipped the country?" Cori kept up the pressure.

"Once again, my genius friend can keep tabs on anyone. Reynolds must think he's safe. Tell the others I'm on my way to his office." Stewart hung up abruptly, as before.

Cori left her office to join the others. They already had decided on something when she arrived. Claris told her about it. "We're going to help Stewart."

"Good." Cori had decided the same thing. "I'm coming too."

Very soon they were on their way to New Haven, where Trent had called ahead to charter a plane to Lehigh, Pennsylvania. A Lyft was waiting to take them to the Key site. The firm was huge, with an outside façade that appeared to be all windows and a greeting area the size of a mall entrance. It spanned several stories and had the firm's name in gold letters the height of an average adult.

Despite what he said he intended to do, Stewart had waited for their arrival and joined them.

"Reynolds is on the third floor."

They proceeded up, and there was another reception area prior to his office entrance. The assistant insisted on announcing them, but Stewart waived her off and barged in while motioning for the others to stay in the waiting area.

Stewart found Reynolds standing over a meeting table sorting through reports.

"Reynolds."

"Montgomery. What are you doing here?"

"I'm here to help."

"With what?"

"Your future."

Reynolds scoffed. "What about my future?"

"Whether you have one worth living, I guess."

Reynolds hadn't been welcoming or friendly, but he became hostile in that moment. "What, are you threatening me with something?"

"No threats, man. Just the facts."

"About what?"

"See these records? Everything we need to put you away for the rest of your life."

"I don't have to tell you that you're just a PI, Montgomery. You can't put anyone away."

"There's a prosecutor outside. I'm ready to give him these documents, and I didn't get the impression he's in any mood to deal. He wants your hide. I'm just here to pave the way to helping yourself out."

"I don't know what you're talking about."

"Evidence, man. Cell records—you tipped off the police in Tashkent. For me, that's a big one. We have locations, IP addresses, among other things."

"If you have all that, and I doubt it, what do you need from me, and what is it that I can do for myself?"

"We've got you cold. You can help yourself by giving us names. It could save us a lot of time and personnel."

"You don't have d**k. You can't imagine the gig businesses involved in this."

"But you can tell me."

Reynolds was near desperation. "I'm not talking to you, you a-hole. Don't you get it?"

A moment before Reynolds started moving toward his desk, Stewart realized he might have a gun and probably would use it. Stewart had a conceal carry permit but wasn't sure how soon he could unholster and scrambled over the desk just as Reynolds reached to open a drawer. He flattened Reynolds to the floor and butt-dialed a pre-planned emergency text to Trent.

"Help. Armed."

Trent flew through the door with a federal prosecutor and special agents in tow, weapons drawn.

This was the best outcome for Stewart. He didn't have to put Trent in an untenable position, nor did he have to use tainted evidence to get Reynolds to talk.

Hours later, one of the investigators emerged from Reynolds's office on his cell. He cited a litany--dozens of names and residences along with associated salons. He was ordering search and arrest warrants. When that call was completed, he made a host of calls to FBI and local police for them to gear up for the raids. He acted as though Stewart and the group didn't exist until Cori spoke up.

"Agent, would you like us to alert hospitals and shelters in the areas affected to respond for the victims?"

"Good thought. I hope the local police and agents will call in services as necessary but let me give you the list in case they need help."

"They will."

Cori and Claris went to work, starting with Blake at Amity, who had immediate access to resources. They went through city by city and divided up the list to make the notifications.

It was midnight before they watched Reynolds taken out in cuffs. They left the building soon after. Trent hadn't retained the plane and pilot, so they all piled in Stewart's rental car for the trip home.

Trent offered to drive, and Stewart and Cori were enthusiastic in taking him up on his offer. Claris and Trent chatted in the front while Cori and Stewart occupied the back and made up for lost time. It was after 5:00 a.m. when they arrived at Cori's apartment. Cori and Stewart took a forced break. Cori invited them in for eggs and toast.

They devoured breakfast with few words spoken. With only a half slice of toast left that no one claimed, Stewart broke the silence.

"Cori and Marga are so much alike it's haunting." He hadn't a chance to debrief the Estonia trip with them. "At first blush, it appears Marga is a bit of a fading violet. Once she becomes comfortable, I can see the intensity increase."

"The scene she set thirty-something years ago in New York was all I needed to understand that Cori and Marga were cut from the same cloth." Trent had a smirk as he added to Stewart's take on their personalities. "In any event, her true willfulness came through in her aching desire to meet you, Cori. She wants to very soon."

Stewart interjected. "I think a destination wedding on Easter weekend at Pirita Beach would be ideal."

The others froze. Cori didn't know if that was a marriage proposal, or a joke, or what it was. She only knew that Stewart was an adrenaline junky.

Stewart broke the stunned silence. "But it doesn't have to be this Easter."

They all laughed, and Cori turned very red. Stewart added, "There will be a romantic proposal without an audience, don't worry. I just want everyone to be prepared."

"I just hope you're prepared for the answer!" Cori gave him the pushback on which he thrived.

Epilogue

The work of these couples would never be done, but that wasn't the criteria they used for inspiration. Their approach was not from a success point of view, but there was rejoicing with each new victim of sex slavery they were able to reach and each new slave holder they were able to identify.

Dr. Rolland Dallas decided it was in his best interest to cooperate with the investigation. He retired rather than lose his license. Cori encouraged the prosecutor to accept a nolo contendere plea with a long probation period on the intimidation charge. His only explanation was he wanted women to have a fresh start and a clean break from their abusers.

Reynolds also cooperated with police but wasn't allowed to plea down enough to escape a prison sentence.

Cori heard a rumor that she had "ghosted" Micah. She made it a point to contact him and asked if that was his impression. He gave her the best news he could. "I'm actually taking Lottie out for dinner tomorrow night. I'm glad to be able to tell you myself rather than your hearing another way."

Cori wished him well. "And think of all the new idioms you'll learn from Louise!"

Della got her puppy, a beagle she named Ruby after Ruby Bridges, and both she and her mom bought a house with a yard suitable for all of them. Reina aced her college courses and caught the attention of a psychiatrist who was a guest speaker at one of her seminars.

Cori did spend Easter week at Pirita Beach, but not as a bride. She met Marga there for the first time. Cori was prepared to let the relationship develop over time and had no expectations of an immediate bond. Yet Marga embraced Cori, physically and emotionally, as most new moms embrace their newborns. The welcome was deferred but was in no way less poignant.

They walked and talked along the beach for hours. Marga wanted to know all about Cori's world. She wanted every detail, and it reminded Cori of her adopted mom's rapt interest in anything, whether boring or otherwise, that Cori was willing to talk about. Cori basked in the attention; she had been too long without a mom.

Marga's interest was in Cori, so she said very little herself. On one of their long walks, she did have something she wanted to tell Cori. "When I was in Finland, I attended a special church with my Finnish family. It was all new to me. Any interest in church was ridiculed during the Soviet era in Estonia, and it has almost vanished from the culture.

"I loved what I heard in that church. The pastor said that heaven was a perfect place, and no wrong-doing could be a part of heaven. What a comfort after the fear and horror I had been through. The pastor said that no one was good enough for that kind of perfection. That wasn't hard for me to believe. It is good that he explained there is a way for us, though we can't be perfect. He said, 'God's wrath against sin' was satisfied by His perfect Son. Most religions tell us what we need to 'do.' In Christ, it already has been 'done.' We only need to trust in His perfect work. Have you ever heard anything like this before, Cori?"

"I have. I have trusted His perfect work. It is the best news ever that you have, too."

Marga was sad to hear about Roman's illness and that his lifetime would be shortened. Marga pored over pictures and assured Cori she would visit her in Connecticut at a time when they could travel to Arizona to see Roman, Ainsleigh, and Helen.

After a few days at the beach, they joined Taavet in Tallinn. Cori's pre-conception of Taavet was way off. She was aware that he was a good deal older than Marga, but he looked, acted and thought like a much younger man. He was an innovator. Rather than stand-offish as Cori had expected, he was full of questions.

Taavet traveled for his work and left them one morning saying he was flying to Stockholm but would return the next day. Indeed, he did, and he had Stewart with him! The four of them went to Pirita for the final weekend in Estonia. On a stroll along the beach on Easter Day, Stewart proposed to Cori. She wanted to be coy and make him wait for an answer. Instead, she said, "I was just about to ask you the same question!" They embraced for a long time. Always one to get the last word, Stewart teased, "Hey, let's have karaoke at our wedding."

Soon after the proposal, Stewart announced he was off to help investigate trafficking among the refugees seeking asylum in European cities. He informed Cori that Claris and Trent were planning to work with non-governmental organizations involved with investigating conditions for the Talibes. She had never heard of Talibes—the boys offered by their families to study the Quran with a teacher or marabout. Stewart explained that the arrangement was mutually beneficial in many situations. Claris and Trent would be in a position to establish practical ways of determining where the practice did not function in a favorable way and to connect the children with resources to help and support them. The work would be important, difficult, and fraught with potential legal and cultural implications.

Marriage with an extractor wasn't going to be a walk in the park, but it wouldn't be dull! Along with Taavet and Marga as major sources of support, Cori initiated plans for a therapeutic shelter in Tallinn on the Gulf of Finland. The name—Seas Inn's Shelter.

CPSIA information can be obtained
at www.ICGtesting.com
Printed in the USA
BVHW040213140220
572392BV00009B/61